MICHELLE'S MIRACLE

A Novella of Romance and Redemption

John Hanson

This is a work of fiction. Names, characters, businesses, places, events, and incidents are either the products of the author's imagination or used in a fictitious manner. Any resemblance to actual persons, living or dead, or actual events is purely coincidental.

ISBN: 978-1-60679-382-4
Library of Congress Control Number: 2017938054
Book layout: Reggie Sugabo
Cover design: Cheery Sugabo
Front cover photo: Sollafune/iStock/Thinkstock
Chapter page photo: NikkiZalewski/iStock/Thinkstock

Healthy Learning
P.O. Box 1828
Monterey, CA 93942
www.healthylearning.com

"There will be more joy in heaven over one sinner who repents than over ninety-nine righteous people who have no need of repentance."

—Luke 15: 7

"As I live, says the Lord, I do not desire the death of the sinner, but rather that he turn back and live."

—Ezekiel 33:11

DEDICATION

To the nurses of the Ochsner Health System

ACKNOWLEDGMENTS

I owe the publication of all three books I have written to the advise and encouragement of Dr. James Peterson of the Healthy Learning publishing company of Monterey, CA. I also have to take my hat off to Dr. Peterson's staffers, Kristi Huelsing, Reggie Sugabo, and Cheery Sugabo, for their editing, layout, and cover design work.

FOREWORD

What is love and what does that have to do with the meaning of our lives? To have this answer is one of the great lessons of life. For Jay Robicheaux, there was another lesson to be learned. In life, sometimes it is not so much the right answer to questions that matters, but the right question that matters.

In this pleasant novella, with a warm cadence that draws you in, we are transported into the story of a derring-do playboy who wrestles with the wild side. Subsequently, we then learn about why asking the right question is far more important even than getting the right answers. He doesn't ask the right question, and so he gets answers with which he may not wish to live.

We are not all Jay. On the other hand, we have either been Jay or we know him, or her. The story unfolds in a Louisiana parish, but its "everyman" aspect is obvious. The dialogue, including the inner dialogue, is real and not filtered. This narrative is not a whitewashed version of our daily reality. One can tell that the era in question is not present-day. The factor that will strike you is that only the details of our daily lives, as well as the technology, have changed. The same plastic and self-satisfying race for nothing continues. While this story repeats itself, rarely do we see a work of fiction that simply and utterly conveys the heart of that empty race. Furthermore, it does so while being entertaining and not being pretentious.

Life is funny. It often uses your existence in ways you could not have expected..and with this story, one must always expect the unexpected. It won't be hard to keep reading. In fact, it might be difficult to stop reading. It will definitely feel like a parting from old friends when the last page has been turned. You'll want to read more…perhaps about the other people in the story…perhaps about our good friend Jay, a fallen angel of sorts whom we find ourselves rooting for and scolding, sometimes in the same breath.

The love story is not obvious. You will see in the end why that is the case. It is a love story we are all called into, and, I might humbly add, it should be the basis of everything in our lives. Our fallen angel friend, with clipped wings and all, seems to limp through his journey, all the while missing the plot, and all the while chasing a prize that is not his to claim! How will he come out?

How will any of it come out? Furthermore, will the price paid be worth it in the end?

—William R. Collier, Jr.
Twenty-Five Year News and Marketing Professional

CONTENTS

1

GAME'S END

Matt Robicheaux's stomach was in a knot. His wife, Mary, held tightly to his left arm with both hands. "Oh, God! Let them score!" she prayed silently. The entire crowd was on its feet now. Matt wondered what his son, Jay, was thinking. There was time-out on the field. Jay had just made the hit that gave his team possession of the ball at their opponent's eleven-yard line. Surrounded by parents of other players, Matt's chest swelled with pride over the game Jay was having, but he could not relax and enjoy their admiration until the drama unfolding below was resolved. Jay's Rummel team was still trailing archrival Brother Martin 9 – 7, with only four seconds to play.

Michelle Delaune stared at the players huddled around Coach Boyle on the sideline. She and the five other cheerleaders were in a tight half-circle now, clinging to one another for support. Donna Beckman, hoarse and exhausted, cried, "This is for district! The playoffs! Oh, I can't stand it!" Michelle never heard a word. Her eyes had found Jay's familiar number and remained riveted on him, as he returned to action with the field goal unit. She wondered what Jay was thinking.

Jay had actually thought fleetingly of Michelle during the break. How he wanted to score with her. He chided himself for his brief loss of concentration. This was the most important moment of his life. He and his teammates had been through hell to have this chance. This was his senior year in high school. He was team captain. He had to lead the way. As he lined up for the snap, Jay looked across the line at the Brother Martin tackle and thought, "Your ass is mine, you son-of-a-bitch."

2

AFTERMATH ON STEWART ST.

Joe Delaune felt good. Everything had gone his way on the tennis court that morning. He had been playing doubles in the same foursome every Sunday morning he could for the past three years. Thoughts of the recent action filled him with a sense of satisfaction and added a special pleasantness to his walk home. He didn't notice the pickup turn onto his street one block ahead and pull up in front of his house.

The sound of the truck's horn jolted Joe from his daydreams, and he looked up in time to see his daughter, Michelle, flash across the sidewalk, hop in the truck, and momentarily embrace Jay Robicheaux. Then, they were off. Jay and Michelle had driven two blocks down Stewart and turned left onto Jefferson Highway by the time

Joe reached his house. Joe wondered why Jay hadn't pulled into the driveway, as he walked toward the rear of his house. Jay always came in and shot the bull for a while.

As he opened the back gate, he realized that Michelle had been wearing Jay's varsity letter jacket. That was a first. It swallowed her, he thought, but Michelle must be on cloud nine. That jacket was one of Jay's most prized possessions.

"How was your match?" Ann Delaune, who was washing some dishes as Joe entered the kitchen, asked. Ann knew from experience that her husband's reply would give her a reading of his mood. She was practiced in the art of giving careful consideration to Joe's mood. She could not stand to fight with Joe and learned early on in their marriage to cope with his many emotional swings.

"Great, honey! Just great!" Joe said with elation. Then, in a suddenly somber tone, he added, "I just saw Michelle and Jay take off, but I never got to talk to them. They never even saw me."

"They were trying to make 11 o'clock Mass," Ann explained. "Jay was running late." Ann sensed that something was wrong. After a "great" match, Joe would talk tennis nonstop for at least two cups of coffee. Something was bothering him.

Joe put his tennis gear on the floor and sat down at the kitchen table. He began sifting through the many sections of the *Times-Picayune*.

"I just made fresh coffee," Ann offered.

"What time did Michelle get in last night?" Joe queried. Ann was taken aback, not only by the question but also by the icy tone of Joe's voice. Struggling to keep her composure, she poured a cup of coffee, sweetened it just the way Joe liked it, and brought it to him. Fear gripped her heart as she remembered how Joe flew into a rage when Michelle missed curfew after a Chapelle school dance last spring. Jay and Michelle were trapped on David Drive until a wreck could be cleared away. Joe was always asleep well before the midnight curfew time, but Ann had made the mistake of telling him about the kids coming in at 1:00 am.

Ann was convinced that if ever God had blessed a couple with a good child, it was Michelle. Ann was deeply hurt when Joe grounded Michelle for a month. Joe had always been sound asleep when Michelle came in and had never in all these months asked the question that now terrified her. By the time she set Joe's coffee before him, she had decided to lie. "Actually, they were in a little early. They were too upset about the game to enjoy themselves."

"Yeah. What a bummer! Here it is in the sports section." Joe sipped his coffee and became engrossed in the sports news.

Ann went back to the dishes. That was a close call she thought. She said a "Hail Mary." It was her way of thanking god for saving her from a very unpleasant domestic crisis. She began to go over in her mind the encounter she had with Michelle when her daughter came home at 2:00 am.

She had quietly slipped out of bed from beside her husband, when she heard Michelle's key working the dead bolt in the front door. Only a mother's ear could have detected that faint sound against the backdrop of Joe's snoring. She met Michelle in the kitchen. She always did. Not only could Ann not sleep until she knew Michelle was safely home, but she never seemed to find time in her daily routines, when she and Michelle could talk with privacy and intimacy. They had both come to savor these dead-of-the-night tete-a-tetes.

"Want some hot chocolate, Mom? It's so cold out." Michelle had been facing the stove, but turned as she finished the question. She moved into her mother's outstretched arms. Michelle hugged her more intensely than usual. She kissed her on the left cheek and began to withdraw, but Ann pulled her back and cradled her head to her bosom. Ann had been so startled by the sight of Michelle's face that she felt faint. She needed the support of this embrace, until she gathered the strength to look into her daughter's eyes again.

Ann's mind flooded. O God! Those eyes! They enraptured everyone. They were the same green as the water along the sugar white beaches of Panama City on a cloudless day. It was not just their beautiful color though. They sparkled so as to appear luminous.

As varied as Joe's moods were, his daughter had but one mood. Michelle was always calmly intense and those shining green eyes projected peace and joy. Suddenly, Ann consciously realized that she had never seen Michelle cry. Not when her Uncle Bob was killed on River Road. Not when her puppy got run over. Not when she broke her wrist in eighth grade. Never a tear. Yet no one doubted her warmth, sympathy, or compassion.

There was no sign of tears in Michelle's eyes just now, but the glow was gone. Holy Mother of Jesus. What was wrong with my baby! The distinctive odor of boiling milk went unnoticed, but the hissing sound emanating from the direction of the stove alerted both women simultaneously.

"I got it, Mom." Turning from Ann's grasp toward the stove, Michelle deftly began to clean up the mess. Ann settled into a chair and leaned against the kitchen table. She wanted to be seated, when she looked Michelle in her eyes. She still did not know why her last look had made her knees buckle.

Michelle thought about her Mom's prolonged embrace, while she fixed some more hot chocolate. Why did Mom cling to her so? She looked like she had seen a ghost. She kept hoping her mother would say something…anything… but Ann remained in uncharacteristic silence. After what seemed an eternity to Michelle, she completed her preparations and brought two steaming mugs to the table.

"Mom, I'm sorry it's so late. It's not Jay's fault." She sat down. Ann cupped her hands around her warm cup and slowly raised it toward her lips. She still had not seen Michelle's face, since that fleeting glimpse before they embraced. She was still trying to fathom why she had been so disturbed.

Slowly, she raised her eyes from her cup to seek the answer. Michelle, seated now, was looking directly at her as she continued. "Jay had me home for twelve, but we sat…just talking…in his truck. We were right out front. I guess I lost track of time. Mom, Jay was so depressed. I just couldn't leave him. Oh, Mom, I love him so much!"

Ann had her answer. She placed her left hand on top of Michelle's right hand, which rested palm down on the table before her. "And I love you, my sweet baby. And don't fret about the time. I really do understand."

Michelle felt a surge of relief. "You're the greatest, Mom!" She noted Ann's gentle smile and thought how lucky she was that her mother was also her best friend. She was glad to see that her mother's color had returned to her face. Michelle told Ann how Jay had let her wear his letter jacket. Ann knew that Michelle should be ecstatic over that, but her daughter spoke only with moderate enthusiasm and only of Jay's reaction to the conclusion of the game while they finished their chocolate.

"Baby, we'll talk again, soon, but I have to get some sleep. Your dad and I are going to 6:30 Mass. Sissy and Bill are going to 9:30." Ann rose wearily.

"Jay's picking me up to go to 11:00." Michelle gave Ann a hug and a kiss. "Goodnight, Mom. I love you."

"I love you, too." Ann spotted the hallway clock as she was leaving. It was 2:30. She turned back to whisper, "Not a word to your father about when you came in."

Ann returned to bed, wondering if Michelle would ever be herself again. She wondered why she hadn't seen it immediately. The change was too sudden…too great…too shocking, she supposed. The light that had burned brightly in her eyes for 17 years was out. It was as if someone had placed filters over them, blocking their lovely radiance. Ann knew that "that someone" was Jay Robicheaux. Michelle's love had made her feel Jay's pain more than he did. It was enough pain to dull the brightest eyes that Ann had ever seen in all of her 54 years on this Earth.

3

SUNDAY SERVICE

The Right Reverend Monsignor John Bennett sat to the right of the main altar. Flanked by two young acolytes, he was enjoying the chance to get off his feet for a few minutes. He had been at St. Matthew's for 24 years and had been its pastor for the last twenty. It wasn't just his feet that were tired.

Sister Joyce Halloran was at the podium, just to the left of center, facing the seated eleven o'clock congregation. The Archbishop permitted her Order to visit each parish once a year and solicit donations for their missions. There was little in Sister Halloran's presentation to hold his attention. Not only had he heard it at the 6:30 service, but he had sat through scores just like it over the many years of his ministry.

A baby began to wail and Monsignor Bennett turned his head and directed a frown toward the disturbance. He watched Mrs. Hazard carry her crying infant down the center aisle toward the small soundproof room just inside the lobby. "Now that's a miracle," he said to himself. "They usually just sit there with their bawling brats, like they were a stage supporting God's gift to entertainment."

Just as Mrs. Hazard approached the "crying room," the large front door opened and a young couple hurried in and stood just inside the entry. Michelle smiled at Mrs. Hazard. The sight of Michelle visibly cheered the Monsignor even though he normally reserved his sternest frowns for late arrivals.

An usher beckoned the couple to move to a vacant spot near the front of the church. Jay found the long walk between the rows of seated worshippers uncomfortable, as everyone who was awake turned their heads away from Sister Halloran toward the couple moving up the aisle. It didn't happen all at once. It began with the people nearest the altar and spread wave-like toward the rear.

As Michelle and Jay advanced, the wave of faces came abreast of them and slowly reflected back to Sister Halloran. She had never seen anything quite like it. She didn't find her voice, until Jay had settled himself beside Michelle. No one but the nun who accompanied her noticed that she had skipped two paragraphs when she resumed her speech.

Michelle had made the walk unaware of the attention that had focused on her and Jay. Her eyes were elevated towards the huge crucifix above the altar. She came to pray, and she was struggling to get her mind to let go of Jay enough to think about God.

Monsignor Bennett never realized it, but it was he who had initiated the wave-like turning of heads. He hadn't even noticed it. From the time he spotted Michelle until she genuflected before entering her pew, his eyes never left her. The people in the front row had simply turned to see what had etched such a pleasant smile on the old pastor's face.

Returning to his much-practiced pose of attention, Monsignor Bennett's mind lingered on Michelle. She was his bright-eyed angel. All of the Delaune children were pretty special to him, but none could hold a candle to Michelle. He had baptized six of the seven Delaune offspring. He had married one and buried another. Three of them were grown up now and living out of the parish. He hoped Michelle would never leave. She was such a unique and beautiful soul. She was like…yes, like a saint…but not hard to live with.

He had talked to Ann Delaune briefly after 6:30 Mass. He had missed Michelle and inquired about her. He knew that the youngest Delaune, 12-year-old Bill, was serving Father Beron's 9:30 Mass and that 14-year-old Sissy would be singing with the choir.

"She'll be coming to eleven with her boy friend, Jay Robicheaux," Ann had explained.

"Tell Michelle to bring him round after Mass. I'd like to meet him."

"I'm sure she will, John. Michelle has wanted you to meet Jay, but he was always involved with football on Sunday mornings. Well, that's all over now…the football. Look, John, Joe's waiting on me in the car. He's itching to play tennis. Have a good one, John."

Monsignor Bennett thought of Ann for a while. They had gone to grammar school and suffered the discipline of the Benedictine nuns together. He thought of the old three-story brick building and the huge church right beside it. Mater Dolorosa. 1200 block of Carrollton Avenue in New Orleans. It was still there. Heavens! Some of those tough nuns were still there!

He really didn't know Ann that well back then. He remembered that she had kissed him once in eighth grade. It was on Marty Fisher's back porch at a King Cake party. Amazing that they would follow such different paths, yet wind up living most of their adult years in the same affluent parish…in River Ridge, a suburban spill-over of New Orleans, not six miles from Mater Dolorosa.

His daydreaming was interrupted as his deacon, Jules Pettijean, intoned, "The Lord be with you!" and his entire flock arose, responding, "And also with you." He was a little irritated to be so suddenly shaken from the comfort of his thoughts and his chair.

Concluding the gospel reading of the day, Deacon Pettijean declared, "This is the Gospel of the Lord!" All replied, "Praise to you, Lord Jesus Christ," and settled back into their seats.

It was sermon time, and Monsignor Bennett was grateful that Deacon Pettijean was delivering it in his stead. He wondered what the 1100 souls in his church thought about during the sermon. His eyes scanned the sea of faces beyond the communion rail and settled on Michelle and Jay. "Michelle is probably the only one here following the sermon," he thought. "I'd like to know what's running through the head of that young man seated beside her."

Jay sat as close as he could to Michelle, his right thigh touching her left, his right arm resting along the back of the bench behind her shoulders. He was still feeling mortified over the stares their late entrance had attracted. His mind drifted to East Jefferson Stadium and to the concluding moment of his last football game in a Rummel uniform. "Damn those Martin cocksuckers! They got more fucking luck! Every year it's the same shit!" he said to himself. "Christ, I hope Ehret kicks their ass in the playoffs." It was as close to praying that Jay had ever come.

Michelle was looking straight at Deacon Pettijean, her hands in her lap. She was struggling to keep her mind on the sermon. She was so happy to have Jay beside her. It was the first time they had been to church together. She recalled the first time they went to a movie. Jay had the two girls working the concession stand in stitches. Michelle's face formed a broad smile, and the movement made her realize she had been distracted from the sermon. "Sorry, Lord," she apologized, and renewed her effort to follow the deacon. She was fighting a losing battle.

In her mind's eye, Michelle was seeing her face in the mirror earlier that morning. After talking with her mom, she had gone to her bathroom to prepare for bed. As she stood before her reflection, the thought of Jay's agony in defeat had overwhelmed her, and a single great teardrop had moved slowly down her left cheek to the corner of her mouth. She had been spellbound at the sight. Now, sitting beside Jay, she felt a certain satisfaction with the thought that her first tear had been for the young man she loved so much. She moved her left hand to rest it on Jay's right knee.

Michelle's touch electrified Jay, and he allowed his right hand to leave the backrest and lightly touch her right shoulder. Jay thought about how Michelle had kissed him when he picked her up for church. Her lips were still as soft and warm, as they were when she comforted him outside her house just hours earlier. It was a softness and warmth that had never been there before last night. Maybe she was loosening up... finally. She had actually parted her lips slightly but not enough to invite any explorations by his tongue. Over the months they had been dating, Michelle had gradually allowed him to caress her outer thighs and torso but her crotch had remained off limits.

She kept his fingers on the outside of her clothes, and she kept her clothes on. It was the way Michelle controlled him that amazed Jay. She never made him feel "put down" or "pissed off," like some other girls. In fact, he looked forward to being with her more and more. Until he met Michelle, he had never continued dating a girl if she wouldn't "put out." Now, he was seeing all he could of this girl, who had him watching his language and going to church and would never "put out" until her wedding night. "Damn!" Jay said to himself. "I must be going crazy!"

After Mass, Michelle introduced Jay to Monsignor Bennett, as he greeted his parishioners departing through the main entrance. "Monsignor Bennett, this is Jay Robicheaux."

The priest embraced Michelle and kissed her gently on her forehead. Then he extended his right hand to Jay. "I'm pleased to meet you, son. Michelle speaks highly of you."

Jay shook hands. "Nice to meet you, Father."

"What parish are you from, Jay?"

"Er,...er..." Jay, embarrassed, struggled to recall. Michelle, however, quickly answered, "Jay's from St. Benilde."

"Yeah, St. Benilde," Jay affirmed. He hoped Monsignor Bennett didn't ask him any more questions about his parish. He didn't even know who was the pastor at St. Benilde. He hadn't been near his parish church in five years.

"Bye, Monsignor," Michelle said, leading Jay down the steps. They would create a bottleneck if they lingered any longer. Jay was grateful to escape any further scrutiny by the Monsignor. As Monsignor Bennett walked back to the sacristy, he thought about Jay and Michelle. He wondered if he would marry them. He had seen hundreds of young couples in love in his career.

He stopped before the altar and knelt. "Please, Jesus, let Jay turn out to be a decent, loving man for my bright-eyed angel." He knew that Michelle was one of those rare persons who fell in love only once, but totally and forever. Her life could be shattered by an unrequited love.

The Monsignor shuddered at the awful premonition induced by his thoughts. He rose and exited the church through the sacristy. Lighting a cigarette, he inhaled deeply and walked toward the rectory, puffing and coughing all the way. "I've got to quit smoking," he said to the statue of St. Matthew in front of his residence.

4

THE SCHOLARSHIP

Mary Robicheaux slumped into her favorite chair in the den with a great sigh. Matt and Jay had just left to go deer hunting. It was only the Friday after the disastrous Rummel loss to Martin, and Mary was delighted to see how the prospect of the hunt had lifted the spirits of her men. Mary could not understand how football and hunting could be so important to them.

Matt and Jay had run her ragged Thursday evening. Matt wanted everything packed and ready to go, when Jay got home from school Friday. Of course, neither Matt nor Jay seemed to be able to find anything in the house. How would they ever find a deer in the woods she thought? At any rate she was glad to have them out of her hair. She also savored the opportunity to relax and not have to take care of anyone but herself for a while.

"When are you coming back?" Mary had asked, as Matt and Jay were going out the door.

"If we kill a buck tomorrow, we may come in Sunday evening. If not, we may stay all week," Matt replied.

"You won't be home for Thanksgiving?"

"Dammit, Mary! Don't worry about it. If we are back, we'll eat out."

Recalling the perfunctory departing kiss Matt gave her, Mary adjusted her recliner all the way back, closed her eyes, and said aloud, "I hope they don't see a damn deer till next Friday."

Mary slept like a baby till the phone awakened her. "Shit!" she said, as she struggled back to consciousness and reached for the phone. The clock next to the phone read 5:15. She had been out for an hour and a half.

"Hello."

"Hi, Mrs. Robicheaux. This is Coach Boyle. Is Jay home?"

"No, Coach."

"How about Matt?"

"They left to go deer hunting. I don't know exactly when they'll be back. They're determined to stay through Jay's whole Thanksgiving break, if that's what it takes to get a deer."

"Well, I have terrific news for the Robicheauxs. Jay has a lock on a football scholarship to USL in Lafayette. Coach Prudhomme just called me. He definitely wants Jay to play for the Raging Cajuns. Of course, Jay will have to meet the minimum academic requirements of the NCAA. That shouldn't be a problem.

"Gosh, Coach Boyle! That's wonderful! They are going to be so exited. I can't wait to tell them. Oh. Would you rather I let you tell them?"

"No. Go ahead and spring it on them. Just have them call me as soon as they get back. Congratulations, Mrs. Robicheaux. You must be proud of your fine young man."

"Thank you, Coach Boyle. Thank you for all you've done for Jay these past four years. You're to be congratulated too…and…please…call me Mary."

"Thank you…Mary. I'll be talking to all of you soon."

"So long, Coach." Mary cradled the phone and lay back in her chair. She barely knew Coach Boyle. This was the most she had ever spoken to him. She thought his voice was extremely sexy. Most of the times, she had watched him as he was standing along the sidelines with his back to her, as she sat in the stands at one or another football stadium. She thought he had the cutest buns. She wondered what it would be like to make love with him. She relaxed and thoroughly enjoyed her fantasy.

5

THE MATCH

Michelle was having a hard time concentrating. She would not have entered this tournament, if Jay had stayed in town for the holidays. She wondered what Jay was doing at this very moment on this opening day of the deer season. She knew he was deer hunting, but nothing in her experience could enable her to relate to that activity.

"Ready, Michelle?" asked her opponent, Susan Mays. Susan's query interrupted her effort to picture Jay in the woods with Bambi.

"What? Oh, sorry. Sure." Michelle rose from the bench, where she and Susan rested on their changeovers. She grabbed her racket and headed for the baseline.

"Two serving three," Susan called out, as she readied herself to serve.

Joe Delaune was disturbed with the way Michelle was playing. She was seeded number three in the girls 18s and received a bye right into this quarterfinal match, but she was struggling to put the Mays girl away. Without taking his eyes off the action, he whispered to Ann, "I don't know where her mind is, but she better get it on this match."

Ann Delaune, seated immediately to Joe's right, whispered back. "She'll be all right. She won the first set, and she'll win this one. Susan hasn't beaten Michelle in three years."

"Michelle never double faults. Five of them today! So far!"

"But, she has held every service."

"Look at all her unforced errors. She has a ton of them. It's just not like her to be sloppy. She's going to fool around and lose."

Another spectator, three rows down, turned to look at Joe for a moment.

"Joe, lower your voice. Better, let's just not talk about the match until it's over. You're getting too worked up, and it won't help Michelle anyway."

Ann knew what Michelle's problem was. Love may be a "many splendored thing," she thought, but it makes it very tough to focus on anything but the beloved. Ann was just happy that the light in Michelle's eyes was again burning brightly. Men never seemed to notice the important things. She wondered if Joe even knew what color her own eyes were.

During the changeover following the seventh game, Michelle used the thought of how happy and excited Jay had been about his pending hunting trip to buoy her spirits and, imaging that Jay was sitting with her parents, she said to herself, "These next three games are for you, my love."

Joe was beside himself as Susan prepared to serve the eighth game, now leading 4 − 3 after breaking Michelle. "She's giving it away!" he exclaimed under his breath, glancing at Ann.

Ann put her forefinger to her lips to silence him. Then, she whispered assuringly, "She'll win. Straight sets."

"Ready? Four serving three!" Susan checked before serving. It was a beautiful slice serve, near the alley side of the deuce court. Michelle moved diagonally toward the path of the ball and drilled it down the line into the corner. Susan could only admire the clean winner. She knew Michelle was back, and she was in trouble.

As the girls shook hands at the net at the end of the match, Susan said, "Wow! If you had played like that from the start, we could have saved a lot of time. Good luck in the semis."

Michelle put her arm around Susan's shoulder. "Good match. You're still in the doubles, right?"

"Yeah. Lisa, and I get to play those girls from Mobile. They're number two seed."

"Hang in there. I'll see you around."

Joe stood up and inhaled deeply. "Did you see that, Ann? Michelle only lost two points in the last three games! That's my girl! I told you she would win!"

Ann just smiled. Joe was Joe, and she loved him. "Let's get a hamburger," she suggested.

6

A DAYDREAM FOR A RAINY DAY

The day before Thanksgiving it rained heavily and turned cold. Nearly all the members of the Black Oaks Hunting Club stayed in camp. Most of them played poker and swapped stories. Several relaxed in their bunks. A few plotted strategies. "Jay, I think we ought to try the bottom between Salt Lick road and Old Well road. You can set up in stand 19 at the south end, and I'll set up in 13 at the north end. We'll get on stand about a half hour before daybreak." Matt paused. "Son, are you listening?"

"Yeah, Dad. I'm on 19 half hour before daybreak," Jay said sleepily.

"Right. Now, stay there till I come for you. I'll start moving slowly down the bottom towards you at 9:00. I should reach you about 10:00. Be sure you don't shoot me!

Hopefully, I'll push a buck out ahead of me, and you can nail him." Matt waited for Jay to comment, but he just lay in his bunk, staring at the ceiling. "Well, what do you think?"

"Sounds OK." Jay was fast losing enthusiasm for deer hunting. Its macho image had been alluring to him, but it was a lot more difficult than football, beer drinking, or womanizing. He had spent the better part of the last four days sitting in trees, trying to be still, quiet, and alert, while squadrons of mosquitoes attacked him relentlessly. He hadn't so much as seen a deer. He was not a quitter, however, and he would keep trying if Dad would.

"It will be better tomorrow, Jay. This front will be through here by early morning. That should get the deer moving around and be the end of the mosquitoes."

"Great," Jay said. "No more mosquitoes, but I get to freeze my balls off."

Matt had to laugh. "Just use the thermal underwear we brought along and all that other cold weather gear. Look, I'm getting into a poker game. See you at supper."

Jay closed his eyes. He knew Matt would be pretty well drunk by suppertime, but he would be cold sober when it came time to hunt tomorrow. It was the same at home. He would start drinking after work and go to bed quite stoned every night. But, he was always ready to go to work in the morning. He was an electrical contractor, specializing in residential wiring. Jay had helped him for a couple of months during the summers following his sophomore and junior years. He had learned enough to know he didn't want to be an electrical contractor.

Jay thought about an "on-the-job" incident that had occurred last July, about a month before the start of fall football practice. As he recalled the sequence of events, a small grin formed on his face and gradually widened into an expression of intense satisfaction. With his eyes shut, he looked every bit the part of the cat that had just swallowed the canary. Jay remembered how he and Matt had gone on a job in the 1800 block of Division St. It was only three and a half blocks from their house in the 1700 block of Turnbull.

"Good morning, Betty."

"Good morning, Matt."

"This is my son, Jay. Jay, this is Mrs. Hensley." Jay just nodded. She was a knockout, he thought. She was wearing cut-off jeans and a purple T-shirt, with LSU printed in gold across the front. What a front! She looked to be about 30.

"Hi, Jay," Mrs. Henley had said with hardly a glance. She was looking at Matt with rapt attention.

"Damn!" Jay had thought to himself. "Dad must have made quite an impression on her when he bid this job. They are already on a first name basis and making goo-goo eyes at each other."

"Let me fix you a cup of coffee, Matt," Mrs. Hensley offered. "How about you, Jay? Coke? Pepsi?"

"No, thanks."

"Black, two sugars. Right, Matt?"

"Right. Look, Jay. Bring in those four ceiling fans and my small toolbox. Oh, yeah. And the six-foot ladder. You can start unpacking one in the master bedroom at the end of the hall."

Jay went to the truck, while Matt followed Mrs. Hensley to the kitchen. "That bitch even knows how my Old Man likes his coffee," he noted.

When Jay finished, he walked to the kitchen door and saw that Mrs. Hensley was pouring Matt a second cup. She rested her left hand on his left shoulder, as she leaned around his right. They hadn't noticed Jay.

"Anything else, Dad?" Jay's voice startled Mrs. Hensley, and she jerked her left hand from Matt's shoulder, like it had suddenly become red hot. Her right hand moved off course, and Matt shot to his feet, his crotch and right thigh soaked with hot coffee.

"Oh, Matt! I'm sorry!" Mrs. Hensley was dapping at Matt's pants with a crumpled paper towel. "I never heard him coming. He was just suddenly there."

Matt was steaming in more ways than one, but he calmly consoled Mr. Hensley. "Many a running back has said the same thing. Jay does move like a cat. There now. It's nobody's fault."

Jay had just stood in the doorway, taking in the whole scene. For all his expression revealed, he might have been looking at a page in his playbook, but it had taken all the self-control he could muster to keep from busting out laughing.

"Matt, I'll get you a pair of Pete's shorts and pants. You're the same size."

"Where is Pete?" Matt inquired.

"Baton Rouge. Won't be home till Saturday morning," Mrs. Hensley replied. Jay stepped aside as Mrs. Hensley passed. He watched her buns move, as she went down the hall. Dad had good taste. As she came back towards him, Jay established his first eye contact with Betty Hensley.

"Go in the bathroom and get out of those wet things right away. I want to wash them before the stain sets up." Mrs. Hensley handed the clothes she had brought from the bedroom to Matt.

"Jay, run home and get me a change. I don't mind using Pete's pants for most of this job, but later I'll need to crawl around in the attic."

Jay left without a word. He had sat behind the steering wheel before he realized the key was not in the ignition. He hurried back into the house. As he approached the bathroom door, he noticed it was slightly ajar. He instinctively froze as he heard Mrs. Hensley laughing softly and realized she was in the bathroom with Matt. Matt's voice came to him loud and clear. "I know you wanted to get me out of my pants, Baby, but…" Matt never finished the sentence, as he and Betty burst out laughing. Jay thought to himself, "Not bad, Dad." He quietly moved back outside, locking the front door. Then, he rang the doorbell. He waited a minute and rang it again. Betty opened the door just enough to see who was there.

"Yes?...Oh, Jay, I thought you were gone."

"I must have locked myself out. I need the truck keys."

"Just a minute." She returned quickly. "Here they are."

Matt and Jay finished the Hensley job about 3:00 that afternoon, and Matt gave Jay the rest of the day off.

Resting on his bunk at the hunting camp, the grin on Jay's face was nearly as wide as it could get. He was getting to the best part.

He had returned to Betty Hensley's house Friday night, just after dark. He walked so no one would notice his truck. He knew Matt was drunk and sound asleep in his Lazy Boy. Mr. Hensley, he recalled was still in Baton Rouge. He might just get lucky. No one answered the bell at first, but he had persisted. Her car was there…lights were on all over the house…the stereo was playing. Finally, Betty spoke through the door.

"Who is it?"

"Your friendly electrician."

Betty fumbled with the lock and then swung the door open. The big smile on her face collapsed when she recognized Jay.

"God! You sound just like your father." Too late now. She had said it. She blushed, as Jay strode across the threshold, grinning at her predicament and thinking how she had put her foot in her mouth. He only had to keep her off balance he thought.

"Expecting Dad?" he teased. Betty shut the door and stood for a moment, with her back to Jay, desperately trying to gather her wits. She was totally off-guard, when she had opened the door. She was in the shower, when the bell had rung and had only put on her bathrobe and wrapped her hair in a towel. She decided to attack.

"What the hell are you doing here?" she said angrily, still facing the door.

Jay ignored the question. He was moving down the hall toward the master bedroom.

Betty whirled around in time to see Jay enter the bedroom. She hurried after him. "Goddammit, Jay, where do you think you're going?"

When Betty confronted him, Jay was sitting on the side of the bed looking right at her. He had the most mischievous blue eyes she had ever seen. He was toying with her she thought. She couldn't shake the thought that somehow Jay knew about her affair with Matt, and her heart sank.

Jay quickly confirmed her worst fears. "How long have you been fucking my Old Man?"

Betty sank to her knees in front of Jay and sat back on her heels. "Jay, please don't tell anyone about Matt and me…ever. You'll wreck…" Jay cut her off in mid-sentence, placing his right index finger across her lips. The grin was gone. Gently, he asked, "You're scared I'll tell?" Betty nodded. "Well," he continued, looking directly into her eyes, "There's one thing we can do to make sure I won't tell."

The worried look on Betty's face slowly changed into a smile, as the implication of Jay's words sank in. She breathed a sigh of relief and lowered her eyes. She felt grateful to Jay, even though he had manipulated her into the sack. "You little devil!" she thought.

"How about a beer?" Jay asked.

Betty rose and kissed him on the forehead. "Yes, Sir!" When she came back she sat a tall glass on the nightstand and emptied a can of Budweiser into it.

"Good thing I didn't order hot coffee," Jay deadpanned.

Betty looked puzzled for just a split second, before she cracked up. "You had to remind me!" she said between giggles.

Aping Matt, Jay repeated what he had overheard him say to Betty in the bathroom last Tuesday. "I know you wanted to get me out of my pants, Baby, but…"

Betty froze momentarily, her mouth agape, her eyes wide with incredulity. Then, she laughed so hard she nearly doubled over. Jay grinned and emptied his glass with one long swallow. Standing up, Jay pulled his T-shirt over his head and dropped it on the carpet. He stepped out of his loafers and dropped his pants. As he removed his briefs, Betty stopped laughing and unwrapped the towel from her head. Then, she shed her bathrobe and went to Jay. "Like father, like son," she said. Jay stayed in his bunk till Matt called him for supper. He had finally dozed off into a deep sleep. Matt sat on the side of his bunk. "I'd like to know what you were dreaming about. You should have seen the smile on your face."

Jay quietly and dryly said, "I was thinking about that big buck we're going to get tomorrow."

7

CONGRATULATIONS

Ann Delaune served Joe a cup of coffee and joined him at the table. Joe hadn't had much to say about his Sunday morning tennis ritual this week and had quickly become engrossed in the sports pages of the *Picayune*. Ann took a sip of coffee and reached for the *Dixie-Roto Magazine*. She had just turned the cover page, when the phone sounded. "Never seen it to fail. There must be some connection between Ma Bell and my fanny. She sure won't let me sit on it." Ann got up. She could drop hints till the cows came home. Joe would never answer the phone, if she were present.

"Hello."

"Michelle home?"

"Jay?"

"Yes, Ma'am."

"Michelle is at Children's hospital. You know. Key Club."

"Oh. Would you tell her I called?"

"Of course, but wait, Jay. How was your trip? Ann stretched the 25-foot phone cord nearly to its maximum length, as she returned to her chair.

"It was OK. We didn't kill a deer though. And we stayed till yesterday evening."

"I'm sorry. You must be disappointed."

"Not really. My mom had great news for me when we got in. I would have called Michelle but it was late. Jay paused for effect. "I got a scholarship to USL."

"Jay, that's wonderful!" Ann reached over and squeezed Joe's wrist. "Joe, Jay got a scholarship to USL!"

Joe extended his right hand. "Let me talk to him." Ann passed the receiver to Joe. "Jay, Joe Delaune. Congratulations. Your dad must be some excited."

"Yes, Sir. Thank you, Mr. Delaune.

"What about his mom?" Ann said under her breath. Ann thought, while Jay's dad would strut around like a peacock now, who has been washing those dirty uniforms all these years?

"Incidentally," Joe said, his chest expanding, "Michelle will probably be getting a tennis scholarship. The coaches from both UNO and Tulane watched her in the Beach Club finals last weekend. They really came to watch that girl from Memphis, who is ranked number two in the South…but, you guessed it…Michelle pulled the big upset. Both coaches talked to her after the match." "That' great, Mr. Delaune. I hear you're quite a player yourself."

"I do all right. Well, let me let you go. We'll tell Michelle you called." Joe extended the receiver to Ann as he returned to his paper. Ann returned it to its place, with a sigh of resignation. She knew she had her man too spoiled for him to even think about getting off his own butt.

8

A SPECIAL VISIT

"Michelle, I want you to visit with a different patient today," Father McCormick said. He had already matched the other Key Club members with patients, and they had scattered throughout the buildings and grounds of Children's Hospital. "Let's sit here a moment." He directed Michelle to a bench across the hall from the chapel entrance.

Michelle looked attentively at the young chaplain from St. Stephen's—Father Mac, they called him. Working with children in pain was wearing him down she thought.

"This patient is a 14-year-old boy. He's in a body cast. He has the use of his arms and upper body, and the doctors expect he'll walk again, but it may take a year or so. The real problem is depression. If we can't turn him soon, he will lose the will to recover. He was a promising junior tennis player. Name's Carl Miller. So, I thought you might know him."

"I know of him, Father. I've seen him at a few tournaments, but I've never met him."

"Come on. I'll introduce you." Room 315 was a cheerful enough room, and the bed was positioned so that the patient had a view of the Mississippi river just over the levee beyond the hospital playground.

"Carl I'd like you to meet Michelle Delaune. Michelle, this is Carl Miller." Carl looked straight at Michelle but said nothing.

Michelle took Carl's right hand in her own and clasped it firmly, but gently. "Hi, Carl. I'm really pleased to meet you."

"You two get acquainted. I'm going for a smoke." Father McCormack stepped just outside the room and lit a cigarette. He left the door open a crack. He wanted to monitor Michelle's visit in case she needed support.

Carl thought to himself that he had never seen someone so beautiful. He looked into Michelle's emerald-like glowing eyes and felt the warmth of her affection embracing him. Michelle continued to hold his hand but said nothing. She communicated to Carl by her gaze and touch that she was there to listen, when and if he had anything to say to her.

Father McCormick wondered if Michelle would ever say anything. He didn't expect Carl would. He was lighting a second cigarette, when he heard Carl speak. "I saw you play in Covington." Father McCormick fumbled his cigarette, burning himself as he tried to catch it. It fell to the tile floor, and he crushed it under his shoe. "Holy shit!" He hissed. Carl's voice had struck him like a bolt from the blue.

"God, Michelle, what a backhand!" Carl continued. You won the girls 18s."

"Thanks. It was a good tournament for me. Did you play that one?"

"Lost to Tom Farris in the finals of the boys 14s."

"So it was a good tournament for you, too."

"It was my last tournament."

"Before your accident?"

"Before or after. I'll be lucky if I can walk when I get out of this thing."

"You'll walk, Carl. It'll be hard at first. Then, when walking is easy, you'll go through the same thing with running. Probably take a year."

"I'll be so behind."

"Just like me."

"What do you mean?"

"Broke my wrist when I was in 14s. I couldn't hold a racket for months. Had to change my grip and all. God works things out for the best though. I had a much better backhand than ever when it was all over."

"How long were you out?"

"Almost a year to the day."

"And look at you now. What a comeback!"

"When you're ready to start working out again, I'll be happy to hit with you."

"Really?"

"Is the Pope Catholic?" Carl's eyes brimmed with tears. "You're very special, you know?" Michelle continued.

"How you figure?"

"I mean God must love you in a special way. He only asks the people he loves the most to bear a heavy cross like yours. People who will take it. He couldn't trust just anyone with it. He picked you out."

"I never thought of it that way."

"Sure. God loved Mary above all humans, and He gave her the heaviest cross of all. The Church calls her the Mother of Sorrows, not just Queen of Heaven. Come on. We'll pray together. She'll help you carry your cross, too, and you'll come back stronger than ever."

Michelle gathered both of Carl's hands in hers and began, "Hail, Mary, full of grace."

Carl joined in. "The Lord is with Thee." Outside the door, Father McCormick prayed with them. When they finished the prayer, the chaplain quietly entered the room.

"Look I have to go now, but I'll be back to see you soon. I'll bring some tennis magazines and a ball to squeeze. We'll talk strategy."

"Promise?"

"Cross my heart!" Michelle leaned over and kissed Carl on the forehead. "See you, Carl."

"Bye, Michelle." Carl paused, then added, "Bye, Father."

"Bye, Son." Father McCormick, numb with emotion, let Michelle pass and turned to follow her out. Carl's voice froze the priest in his tracks. "Father!"

The priest looked back at Carl. "Yes?"

Carl was smiling. "I'm special."

"You are indeed, Carl."

In the hall, the chaplain lit a cigarette, as they walked away from room 315. A great lump had formed in his throat, and his nose was running. Finding it impossible to inhale, he snuffed out his cigarette. He leaned against the wall and wept. He said to himself, as he battled to regain his composure, "And I stood by the door in case she needed my support! Oh, God! Out of the mouths of infants...."

Michelle put her hand on his shoulder. When he turned his wet, reddened face toward her, she handed him several tissues from her purse. "Thanks." He used the tissues and took a big breath. "I want you to know, Michelle. Carl has been at Children's for three weeks and just now was the first time he spoke to anyone."

Michelle just smiled. She has the aura of an angel the priest thought.

"Come on, Father Mac. I'll get you a cup of coffee." She started down the hall toward the nurses' station.

"There goes the greatest argument the Church will ever have for ordaining women," he said to himself.

9

SCHOOL SPIRIT

Jay sat in the student section of the Rummel gym, facing the cheerleaders. On his right sat Scott Weigand, his best friend. Scott was a senior, too, and had played weakside linebacker along side Jay for two years. Across the court, Coach Boyle sat in a thinly populated section near Mr. Rohr's jazz ensemble. From that vantage point, he could see which of his football players had come out in support of the basketball team, a practice he strongly encouraged. It was all part of Raider pride, which helped make Rummel's sports program one of the most successful in all of Louisiana.

"Where yat, Coach?" Coach Boyle saw Larry Simkin bounding up several rows to join him, his right hand extended. He smiled. He was always delighted to see his former players attend Rummel athletic events.

"Long time no see, Coach! How you been?"

"Can't complain. How's Tech?"

"One more semester, and I'm out. I graduate in May. I have a 3.0 GPA in civil engineering."

"That's great. Coming back to this area?"

"I don't know yet. But, I've had enough of Ruston. Looks like you have a lot of your players out tonight." Larry was looking across the court at the student section. He saw a lot of football letter jackets.

The teams were still warming up, and the jazz band was blaring out a lively rendition of "Sweet Georgia Brown." Just as they finished, one of the seniors near the top of the student section yelled, "Come on, Jay! Give us a cheer!"

The other seniors picked up on it, and soon the whole section was urging Jay on. He didn't need it. Jay stood up, cupped his hands over his mouth and began in a loud bass voice, "Rah! Rah! Rah!"

"Rah! Rah! Rah!" the students echoed.

"Hit 'em in the knee!" Jay bellowed.

"Hit 'em in the knee!" More students had joined in now.

Michelle looked at Donna, then at Jay. "What now," she thought.

"Rah! Rah! Rass!" Jay thundered.

"Rah! Rah! Rass!," the Rummel crowd screamed. Brother Peter, the cheerleaders' moderator, shot to his feet and winced apprehensively.

Jay raised both fists above his head. Pausing, he basked momentarily in the attention of his peers. Then, flashing his inimitable devilish grin, he winked at Brother Peter and roared, "Hit 'em in the other knee!"

It was a few minutes before the cheerleaders could get the students to follow them in a standard cheer.

"Who is that guy, Coach?" Larry Simkin asked.

"That's our All-State linebacker, Jay Robicheaux."

"Shy rascal, huh?" He looks strong as an ox. How big is he?"

"Jay is six-foot, 210 pounds. Under 9% body fat." The kid next to him, Scott Weigand, is five-ten, 195."

"Did they get scholarships?"

"Jay did. USL."

"I don't remember the cheerleaders being that pretty, when I was here. Who's the third girl from the left? She's gorgeous. Built like a brick shit house."

Coach Boyle paused, suppressing a grin. "That's Michelle Delaune. She's Robicheaux's girl friend."

"Lucky devil. You know, Robicheaux could pass for 22."

"From what I just heard from a reliable source, he has. The word is that no bar in Fat City or the Quarter has asked him for an ID, since his freshman year. Now, they tell me!"

* * * *

At half-time Rummel led Holy Cross 35 – 24. Michelle had gone to the ladies room with Donna Beckman. Jay and Scott waited for cokes at the concession stand.

"I hear you're helping out with spring football," Scott said to Jay.

"Yeah. Coach Boyle asked me. It's just three weeks."

"What about track? What did Coach Johnson say?"

"He was so grateful to Coach Boyle for going to bat for me with Mr. Bostick, he would have kissed his ass. That fag was going to flunk me over some fucking term paper. I would have been ineligible. Coach Boyle talked Bostick into letting me do it during the Christmas holidays."

"Damn, Jay."

"Get this. I had to make an A on the term paper just to make a lousy D for the semester."

"You made an A? Come on, Jay! Who you kidding!" "Well, Michelle helped me a little."

"A little? Just a little, huh?

"Yeah. The fag made me pick one of three topics." Jay grinned. "I picked the right one, I guess."

Scott laughed. "So, Coach Johnson lets you skip track practice for three weeks?"

"He gave me a workout schedule. I do it after football drills. Hell, I've been throwing the shot and discus for three years now. I'll be ready."

Michelle and Donna sat on a bench directly across the lobby from the concession stand. Jay and Scott were still waiting to be served, when they came out of the restroom.

Donna motioned toward Jay. "That Jay! I laughed until I cried. Him and his cheer!"

Michelle smiled. "How are you and Scott doing? You looked so nice together at the Winter Dance last Saturday night"

"He's a real pitty-pat, but we're not really steady…yet. But, I'm working on it. We're going to the Crazy Wave by Tulane after the game. It would be neat if you and Jay could come."

"Thanks, Donna, but Tuesday nights are rough for me. I have tennis practice after school, so, I can't study until after the game. My dad wants me home by 10:30 on our Tuesday game nights. Of course, I can stay out to 12:00 after our Friday night games."

"But, Michelle, the games don't finish until around 9:30. Then Brother Peter usually has something to say to us about our cheering. What can you and Jay do?"

"We write off weeknights and try to plan a real nice Saturday date. Any way, Jay really needs to hit the books this last semester. Besides track and his courses, he's sweating the SAT."

"Here come our Cokes. Thank God. I'm dying of thirst."

10

A JOB FOR JAY

After the game Jay and Michelle stopped at the Burger King on the corner of Airline Highway and Division St. They were less than ten minutes from Michelle's house, and it was just 9:50 so they could relax together for a few minutes.

"It looks like I've found the perfect job, Michelle."

"What, Jay?"

"Shoveling shit."

Michelle laughed. Jay was always joking. Her green eyes flashed with curiosity, when no punch line was forthcoming. "What on earth are you talking about?"

"There's this lady over near Kenner who has about 20 dogs. She trains them to find dope. Well, she wants someone to come over and clean her kennels and feed the dogs, either Saturday or Sunday. She doesn't care which day or what time of day. Just so it gets done. I get twenty bucks for maybe an hour and a half, and I get to pick my time. I can't work during the week anyway, with school and all, but this won't affect the amount of time I can spend with you on weekends either. How about that?"

"Shoveling shit, huh?" Michelle teased. "That would be right up your alley, if the lady raised bulls."

11

MONDAY MORNING MEETING

Coach Boyle walked from his office in the field house toward the administration wing of Rummel High School. It was the first Monday morning in February. Monday mornings were always hard he thought, but especially so at this time of year. There just wasn't much happening to break up the monotony of going to class. Since the second quarter exams, they had had three weeks of school without a holiday or an abbreviated schedule.

The faculty mailroom was crowded with teachers checking their cubbyholes or waiting to use the Xerox machine. Glancing through the stack of materials he removed from his box, Coach Boyle found a note from the senior counselor, Dan Fontana.

Simultaneously, he realized that Dan was standing on his right perusing the contents of his own box.

"Morning, Dan. I see you sent me a note."

"Yes, Jim. I need to get together with you as soon as possible."

"How about the beginning of first period?"

"Fine. I'll be in the Guidance Lobby."

Coach Boyle left those of his colleagues still in the mailroom and joined the handful of early arrivals in the faculty lounge. Most of them seemed as zombie-like, as the kids dragging themselves from the long lines of school buses in the parking lot. He sat on the tacky, gray vinyl sofa near the windows and began to go through the materials he had brought from the mailroom. By the time the bell signaling the start of homeroom sounded, he had dumped the entire stack in the wastebasket and fixed himself a cup of coffee. He picked up the sports section of the *Times-Picayune* to help kill the ten minutes until first period.

"Hey, Coach. How about some "hearts'?" Tony Bordes was shuffling a deck of cards at the round table in the center of the lounge.

"I have an appointment first period. Where's Larry?"

"He got a sub."

"Great way to start the week. Who's out?"

"Ms. Perot."

"Again?"

"It's Monday, ain't it?"

"I wonder what her problem is?"

"Let's just say that if she got on the wagon, she could make it to school five days in a row. That is, when we have five days in a row."

"Well, this will be our fourth straight five-day week. We may lose our title of 'Holiday High." Coach Boyle sat at the card table, as the bell ending homeroom rang. He would wait a few minutes to let the halls clear.

"We should just call off school until after Mardi Gras. Hell, they just come to school to sleep. They're either at King Cake parties or chasing parades half the night." Tony began laying down the cards for solitaire, as he spoke.

"Say, Tony. How is Jay Robicheaux doing in your class?"

"A little better. He seems to have settled down some. Did I tell you what happened when the Southern Association team visited last week? One of them…remember the bald guy with the rimless glasses? He asked Jay, who's standing by the door before class, how many students he had. Jay tells him without batting an eye, "I don't teach. I'm the principal.""

Coach Boyle smiled broadly and nodded knowingly. "He's a character. God threw away the mold when He made Jay." Pausing, he raised his eyes toward the ceiling. "Thanks, Lord. One was enough."

"Come on, Coach. You could use a dozen like Jay. He was one hell of a football player for you."

"I couldn't stand the aggravation. It's been a pain keeping him academically eligible for four years. In addition, I was always worrying that he would do something crazy and get himself suspended or arrested. Truth is…I'm glad he came, and I'm glad he's going."

"I hear he's going to USL."

"If he passes the SAT." Coach Boyle stood up, stretched, and yawned. "Gotta run. Have a good one."

Dan sat behind his desk and folded his arms. The counselor seemed uncomfortable under the steady gaze of the coach, as he began speaking very slowly. "Jim, the SAT scores will be distributed Wednesday. I wanted to see you before that because…" Dan paused, searching for the right words. "Well, it's like they say, 'To be forewarned is to be forearmed'. I…er…I…"

Jim cut Dan short. "Are you trying to tell me that Jay didn't make it?"

Dan nodded.

"I see. How bad?"

"That's the pity of it. He missed by two points."

"Damn!"

Neither man spoke for a long moment. Jim Boyle broke the silence. "Thanks for letting me know before the 'shit hit the fan'. You know, I've kind of been expecting it, but you always hope for the best. Look, Dan, is it all right if I let Coach Prudhomme know right away? He'll keep it under his hat and it'll give him two extra recruiting days to replace Jay. Who knows? He might give it to Scott Weigand."

"Sure, Jim. I'm really sorry."

"Thanks for your concern." Jim stood and shook hands with Dan before leaving.

12

A TEAR OF JOY

"Michelle, why don't you and Jay come with us to the Moonwalk. I know you have to get home by twelve, but it's only 9:30, and we're practically there." Donna and Michelle were exiting the Jesuit gym, with Scott and Jay several paces behind them.

Michelle touched Donna lightly on her forearm. "Thanks, but Jay and I need some time alone. He's in no mood to party."

"I guess you're right. I was afraid he was going to get in a fight with that black referee."

"You and me both. That would have been a bad scene. He'll be all right in a couple of days. Right now, he's just mad at the world."

"Present company excepted," Donna smiled. They stopped at the banquet, and Jay and Scott caught up with them.

"Where you parked?" Scott asked Jay. Jay nodded towards Carrollton Avenue.

"We're the other way." Scott took Donna's arm. "Be cool."

The two couples parted and walked in opposite directions along Banks St. Jay put his right arm around Michelle's shoulders, and she reached across his lower back to grasp his left side with her left hand. They walked the two and a half blocks to Jay's truck in silence.

As Jay opened the passenger side door for Michelle, she firmly turned to face him. She put both her arms around his waist and embraced him, pressing the left side of her face against his chest. They stood so for a long moment, partially illuminated by the streetlight filtering through the gigantic live oak between the banquet and the curb.

Jay felt Michelle's breasts yield and settle to the contours of his abdominal muscles. Like a heating pad drawing the soreness from an aching muscle, Jay perceived the warmth of her love engulfing him, siphoning away his rage and pain. A tremendous feeling of well-being permeated his psyche and displaced his turmoil, as he tilted Michelle's head back and peered into her glowing eyes. In that moment, he realized that Michelle had become more important than anything in his life, and nothing could take her away from him.

"I love you," Jay said. He leaned into Michelle's sweet parted lips. A single great tear of joy rolled unnoticed down the shadowed side of Michelle's face.

Several groups of fans drove by honking and cheering, before they ended their embrace. "Come on. Let's go." Jay drove to the lakefront and parked nearly directly across Lakeshore Drive from the Mardi Gras Fountain. He and Michelle walked hand in hand to the sea wall and sat on the top step. Small swells rolled in from Lake Pontchartrain and crashed at the base of the sea wall, sending a briny spray nearly to their feet. "It's beautiful, Jay! I love looking at the fountain from here."

"How about that moon, Michelle?"

"Where?"

Jay pointed past her left shoulder to the western sky, where a bright half moon sat suspended above the Causeway Bridge.

"It's beautiful, too. Everything is beautiful."

"You're beautiful."

"And you, too."

"I wish my folks thought so."

"Of course they do."

"My old man was so mad about me losing that scholarship. He didn't go to work yesterday or today. I wonder if he'll ever sober up. My Mom just cries all day. The wimps around school look at me like I'm some kind of freak."

Michelle noticed that Jay spoke softly and without a hint of rancor in his tone. She knew he was leading up to something, not simply looking for sympathy or venting his frustration, but struggling to find the right words.

Jay paused. He looked lovingly into Michelle's eyes and wondered if he needed any words to share his thoughts with her. She seemed to be looking into his very soul.

"Michelle, I've been such a fool. Except for the time I've spent with you, my life has been a waste. All I wanted to do was play football and party. I never studied. You know, I'm glad now that I lost my scholarship, and I don't care if I never see another football. You opened my eyes tonight, Michelle. I know what I want now, and, for the first time in my life, it's something worthwhile."

Michelle's expression asked the question that Jay's statement invited though her heart already knew the answer.

"You. You, Michelle. I want you to be with me always. I want to care for you and be the father of your children."

Michelle cradled Jay's chin between her hands and kissed him gently. "I'm so happy that we want the same thing. I can't imagine life without you."

They looked at each other for a long moment, before Jay broke the silence. "I don't know exactly what I'm going to do, but I am going to make something of myself. I want you to have the best. I realize it's going to take time and a lot of work. Right now, I can't even buy you a ring."

"We're so young, darling. We have plenty of time. You do what you feel you must. When you're ready, I'll be waiting. Just remember. As long as I have you, I consider myself the richest girl in the world."

Jay took Michelle into his arms, and they held each other cheek to cheek, as in a slow dance. "I wish we could stay like this forever," Michelle whispered.

"Me, too, but I have to get you home by twelve."

13

A MUTUAL ATTRACTION

Jim Boyle sat in his favorite booth at Shoney's. He enjoyed having an early Saturday morning breakfast during the off season, when he could take his time and savor the delights of the breakfast bar. He had the *Picayune* folded to reveal the article in the sports section on last night's Rummel-Jesuit basketball game.

"Y'all win?" Irene, his waitress, offered more coffee.

"Sure did." Jim nodded, and Irene topped off his mug. "Thanks."

"Still single?" Irene winked. Jim just smiled, as Irene moved to the next booth. She was his mother's age and asked the same questions he thought.

The article said nothing about the fight that nearly erupted between Jay Robicheaux and the black official, Lloyd Jackson. Thank God. The school doesn't need that kind of publicity he reflected. Like Jay blowing his scholarship. At least it hasn't been in the paper or on TV…yet. Maybe, we'll be lucky.

"Shit!" Jim exclaimed under his breath. He had adjusted the paper, and his wishful thinking was shattered, as he read a scathing editorial on the overemphasis of athletics to the detriment of academics. It was written by the senior sports editor, Brian Paxton, and he used Jay's situation mercilessly to make his point. "Wait till I get a hold of that son-of-a-bitch," Jim vowed.

Jim left a tip for Irene and stormed toward the cashier's stand with his check.

"Everything all right, sir?" The cashier smiled cheerfully.

"Just fine." Jim's scowl unnerved the woman, and her hand trembled slightly, as she handed him his change. As Jim hurried from the restaurant, she said to herself, "If that's how he is when everything's fine, I pray God we never upset him!"

Jim drove east on Veterans Boulevard to Cleary, where he turned south, crossing the I-10 overpass and the West Napoleon Canal, which formed the northern boundary of the Rummel campus about a mile to the east. He weaved his way along his shortcut through the middle class subdivision that sprawled between Cleary Avenue and the parallel Severn Avenue, which separated Rummel's school buildings from its athletic fields.

During the drive, Jim kept seeing Mary Robicheaux's face in his mind. He had gone to her house Wednesday night after the SAT results were released. He and Mary had talked till nearly one in the morning. Neither Matt nor Jay had come home. He hadn't known what to expect but her voice had sounded so desperate over the phone that his heart had gone out to her.

He felt very responsible in the whole matter and was eager to offer what comfort he could. She had called again Thursday, and they had talked on the phone for nearly three hours. It did wonders for his ego that someone would confide so completely in him, and he took solace in the knowledge that he was able to confide in Mary as well.

As he came to the stop sign at Turnbull, Jim felt overcome by an impulse to see Mary. Instead of continuing straight on 39th St. to the Fieldhouse, he turned right toward the 1800 block and the Robicheaux residence. "Why am I doing this?" he asked himself aloud.

"Jim!" Mary was surprised, but delighted, to see him when she answered the door. "Come in!"

Jim just smiled and followed her to the breakfast nook adjoining the kitchen. On the way, he sought a reason to justify his unannounced visit. "I was just in the neighborhood, and I thought I'd stop and see how ya'll were doing. He decided not to comment on Paxton's editorial if Mary didn't bring it up.

"I'm so glad you did, Jim. Sit down. Can I get you some coffee?"

"No, thanks. I just had some at Shoney's."

"Well, I'm having a cup."

"OK, then, I'll have a little with you."

As Mary readied their coffee, Jim asked, "Where's Matt and Jay?"

"They're gone. As you know, I still hadn't seen Matt since Wednesday afternoon, when I spoke to you Thursday. Well, he came in very late Thursday night and passed out on the couch. Friday morning, he took off for Empire. He said he has a job wiring a fishing camp. I don't expect him back till Wednesday. The man he's working for is supposed to take him fishing Monday and Tuesday."

"You'll be alone on Mardi Gras?" Jim asked sympathetically.

"So, what's new? I was alone Thanksgiving. Remember? The mood he's in now, I'd just as soon he be out of the house." Mary brought their coffee and sat down with Jim.

"How about Jay?"

"Jay's the good news. What a change! I really think he's over his mad."

"Didn't look that way at the Jesuit game last night."

"Well, he was still unbearable when he left for the game. I don't think he would have gone, if it hadn't been for Michelle. But, this morning! Jim, he looked…gosh, the best I can say it…he looked happy…and peaceful. It's like some great weight has been lifted from his shoulders. Before he left he hugged and kissed me. 'Mom,' he says, 'It's going to be all right. I'm fine now. Really. I can face anything.' Those were his very words."

"Where did he go?"

"Michelle invited him to breakfast at her house. Then, they're going to the parades. The one in Metairie this afternoon and the one in New Orleans tonight."

"Well, Mary, you certainly seem to be feeling a lot better. I'm glad to see it."

"Thanks to you, Jim. I don't think I would have made it without you."

"I like to think I helped, but this change in Jay seems to be the big factor. I suspect he has Michelle to thank for that. Let's hope it lasts.

"You're such a sweet man."

"You're such a sweet lady." Jim impulsively reached out and took Mary's hands in his, and their flesh tingled from head to toe. They looked into each other's eyes for several seconds, surprised and speechless at the sudden magic of the moment.

Jim broke the spell, standing as he spoke. "Thanks for the coffee, Mary, but I better get going."

Mary still firmly grasped his left hand. "Please stay a little longer," she pleaded.

"Well, OK. Just a few minutes."

"Let's go where we'll be more comfortable." She led him to the love seat in the parlor. It was nearly 2:30 pm, when Jim Boyle started his car's engine and drove away from the Robicheaux residence.

14

MAN TALK

Jay wiped his lips with a green linen napkin. "That was really good."

"Would you like some more?" Michelle offered. "No, thanks."

"Don't be bashful," Michelle jested.

"I think he's just full, Michelle," Ann Delaune interjected. "Turning down a fourth helping is hardly being bashful."

Jay smiled. He was really feeling at home. Michelle's parents had a whole different kind of relationship than his own. There was a kind of caring in this family that was missing in his own.

"Jay, will you throw the football with me now?" Bill Delaune asked admiringly.

"Sure, Sport. If we have time." Jay looked at Michelle.

"Bill, you have soccer practice. Remember?" Joe reminded. "In fact, you'd better get a move on, or you'll be late."

"Shucks!" Bill rapped playfully on Jay's arm with his fist. "Maybe next time."

"You got it," Jay promised.

"May I be excused?" Sissy asked. "I have a CYO meeting."

"Of course, Dear. Before you go though, give me a hand with the dishes."

Sissy assented, "Sure Mom."

Joe then led them in thanksgiving. Bowing their heads they prayed, "We give thee thanks, Almighty God, for these and all the benefits which we have received from Thy bounty through Christ, Our Lord. Amen." Joe got up from the table and everyone followed suit.

"Honey, we're going over to the courts for a little while. Should be back by quarter to eleven." Joe turned toward Ann, who was opening the dishwasher. "I just want to look at Michelle's serve before they go to the parades."

"Don't forget I need you to help me make groceries at Schwegmann's," Ann said.

"Michelle, you go ahead in the car and get loosened up, while Jay and I walk over. It'll give us a chance to stretch our legs and do some man talk." Joe smiled at Jay.

As they started walking along Stewart towards Little Farms Playground, Joe flatly asked Jay, "Do you intend to marry Michelle?"

"Yes, Sir."

"I see. How do you intend to support her?"

"Relax, Mr. Delaune. Let's get one thing straight. I don't intend to marry her in the near future. I need to get it together and make something of myself. As I see it now, we're looking at four to six years, depending on how things go."

"That's a very mature outlook. A lot of young people won't wait that long."

"It's not that long compared to a lifetime together. And that's what I want for us. I also think Michelle should finish college before we marry. I know she'll finish in four years, but it will probable take me six."

"Why so long?'

"I'm way behind academically, and I don't have a scholarship any more, so I'm going to have to work a while and save."

"Do you have a job now?"

"Right now, I'm going to concentrate on doing the best I can in these last few months at Rummel. I have something to prove. I'm going to make the fucking honor roll." Jay felt a tinge of shame, as soon as he let slip the F-word in Joe's presence.

"The what?" Joe's eyebrows shot up.

"The honor roll."

"Oh."

"So, the only job I have is a part-time one, cleaning some dog kennels once a week."

"How about the summer?" "One of my Dad's customers needs a salesman to work South Louisiana, and he thinks I'd be perfect for the job. It looks like my best prospect for now."

"Do you know what you want to major in when you get in college?"

"Not really, but I'm very interested in law."

"I'm asking a lot of questions."

"I don't mind. I know you love Michelle. I would do the same thing, if I were in your place."

"One more. Are you serious about your religion?"

"I never was, but now it's like on my mind a lot. Michelle has been getting me to Mass on Sundays, since football ended, and she is such a good person. I have a lot of catching up in that area. Religion, I mean. I need time to think."

"You not only need time to think, Jay, but you need a place where you can think, pray, and get some guidance. That takes some special effort. Are you really serious about this?"

"I would do anything for Michelle." Jay immediately regretted putting himself in the position of having to do anything Joe might suggest. Too late now, he thought.

"Good. School is out next week because of Mardi Gras. I'll get you on the list for our men's retreat next weekend. I'm one of the Captains."

"How long is it?"

"About three days. It's a closed retreat. We check in Thursday evening and stay till about 1:00 Sunday afternoon. We can be back by 2:30."

"That will give me time to do the kennels. How much is it?" "It's free. The retreats are supported by voluntary and anonymous donations."

"Put me down, Mr. Delaune. And thanks." Jay did not like being boxed in to this commitment, but showed no hint of his displeasure in his expression. He had to stay on Joe's good side, if he was to have Michelle.

Joe's apprehension was gone. He felt very good about Jay and Michelle for the first time since they had started dating. Manresa retreats had changed many a man's ways.

15

RANCID WRATH

It was 4:30 in the afternoon, when Jay arrived at Jane Gomez's place in Kenner. It had been a long day. Jay recalled attending Sunday Mass with Michelle at the small chapel at Children's Hospital. Afterward, Michelle had introduced him to her young friend in the body cast. Then, he and Michelle had met Scott and Donna for the Krewe of Jefferson Parade in Metairie. Finally, he had brought Michelle home and made his way to the kennels. He knew he would barely have enough daylight to finish.

The kennels were along the south side of Jane's house, and a six-foot cypress fence hid them from the view of passersby on the westbound lanes of West Metairie that bordered a fifty-foot wide drainage canal. Jay unlocked the padlock that secured the small gate Jane had installed in the fence. He had to step through the opening while ducking down. Jay secured the dogs in their sheltered sleeping quarters, and they quieted down.

Then, he began scooping the canine excrement from the spacious concrete runs and loading it into a large black heavy-duty plastic garbage bag. When he finished, the bag held twenty pounds of a malodorous, lumpy blend of dog stools that had the consistency of a thick syrup. Jay was relieved to seal it with a twist tie. "I'll never get used to that smell," he said to himself. Jay placed the bag near the gate in the fence and began washing down the runs with a pressure hose and filling the drinking buckets with fresh water.

Jay had just released the last of the dogs into their runs, when the streetlights came on. It was nearly six, but Jay had only to lock up and take the bag of dung around front to the garbage can.

Swinging the gate outward, Jay stooped, turned, and backed through the opening, carefully lifting the garbage bag after him. He had not straightened up yet, when a strange voice sounded behind him.

"Let's see what you got, Motherfucker!"

Glancing over his left shoulder just enough to employ his peripheral vision, Jay saw a tall, gangly black man. He was wearing a black sweat suit. In his left hand, an opened switchblade flashed menacingly in the glare of the streetlight. In a split second, the realization that he was being mugged filled Jay with rage, and a great rush of adrenaline fueled his reaction. From his semi-crouched position, he exploded upward, whirling with the practiced motion of a discus thrower. The bag in his right hand, like some giant weighted sock, swung up and around Jay in a great arc.

Instinctively, the mugger flung his arms upward to ward off the blow. The blade in his left hand ripped the bag asunder, and its reeking contents inundated his head and shoulders. Blinded and gagging, he screamed, "Shit! Shit!"

"You got that right, you stinking bastard!"

Jay kicked him in the groin, and his assailant doubled over in pain, dropping his knife. Jay grabbed him by the back of his shirt and the seat of his pants and ran, shoving the moaning mugger ahead of him, across West Metairie to the lip of the drainage canal. With a mighty heave Jay hurled him into the huge ditch. The man landed about midway down the steeply sloped north bank and rolled into the muck at the bottom of the nearly empty channel.

Jay wiped his lightly soiled hands on the grass along the curb and observed the would-be-robber struggling to extricate himself from the clinging mire of the canal bed. His face distorted with pain, he shouted at Jay accusingly, "You broke my arm, Motherfucker!"

Jay's stare was icy cold, though he was still afire with anger. "You come back up this side, and I'll break your fucking neck!"

Jay watched as the man struggled up the south side of the canal bank, crossed the eastbound lanes of West Metairie and moved out of sight down Maryland St. "Stinking son-of-a-bitch! Pulled a knife on me! Can you believe that shit."

16

FIELDHOUSE AFFAIR

Mary Robicheaux noticed that the streets of her neighborhood were nearly deserted. She had decided to walk down Turnbull to the West Napoleon Canal and follow the footpath along its south bank to the Rummel campus. Everybody and his dog must be at Mercury or in one of the other area parades she thought. Mardi Gras may be good for something after all. The fewer folks see me, the better.

Jim Boyle had driven to Rummel in the driver's education car furnished to the school by Crown Buick. There was no one in sight, as he parked the Regal in its slot in the breezeway under the gym. He checked his Timex. 12:20 pm. The parade on Veterans would be in full swing and, with the weather so pretty, he figured the turnout would be tremendous. None of the coaches would come here this Sunday afternoon, and the Brothers had deserted their residence on campus, either to party with their confreres at De La Salle or to relax at their camp on the Tchefuncta River. He and Mary could count on being undisturbed until at least midnight. Plenty of time for a lover's tryst.

At 12:55, Mary approached the north entrance to the windowless concrete-block edifice that was the Rummel Fieldhouse. Jim had unlocked the metal door for her and was waiting just inside as they had planned. As she closed the door behind her, Jim locked it and swept her into his arms.

"Wait, Jim." Mary gently withdrew after a long passionate kiss. "Let me put my purse down."

"Here. Let me have it. I'll put it in my locker."

Mary removed the top half of her hooded sweat suit. "Take this, too."

"No one would recognize you in that outfit, Mary. Especially with those sunglasses."

"I wore them, too. I needn't have bothered. All I saw coming over was the Wilson's pooch. The whole world must be at the parades."

"Typical Mardi Gras madness. Well, it'll all be over by Wednesday. Where did you park?"

"I left my car home. I thought it would be safer. Can't be too careful. Anyway, I like to walk. How 'bout you?"

"I used the driver's ed Buick. No one passing by will have a clue that we're in here. We can even put some music on. It can't be heard from outside."

"I have a feeling we'll be making our own beautiful music." Mary moved to embrace Jim. She placed her right cheek against his chest and wrapped her arms tightly around his waist. Jim cradled her head in his huge hands and gently ran his fingers through her hair. After a moment Mary slid her hands down from Jim's waist and playfully squeezed his buttocks, turning her face upward to savor his reaction.

Jim smiled and moved his mouth to her parted lips. Mary closed her eyes and sighed contentedly as Jim's lips closed softly on her lower lip near the right corner of her mouth. Slowly, gently squeezing and releasing, Jim kissed her along the entire length of the lip to the left corner of her mouth. He traced a trail with tender kisses up her left cheek and temple, across her forehead, and down the right side of her face to just beneath her right ear. From there, he kissed his way diagonally down the side of her neck to a point under her uplifted chin.

Mary became pleasurably aware of the seepage in her crotch as Jim's kisses progressed up the left side of her neck and completed the circuit to the left corner of her mouth which was now half opened. Jim inserted the tip of his tongue and moved it around the perimeter of the orifice outlined by Mary's lips. From time to time, as his tongue repeated the route, Mary drew it in more deeply and held it with a firm suction before slowly releasing it. Finally, they rested, holding each other cheek-to-check.

"Oh, Jim! You can't imagine what pleasure you give me. You've got me all wet."

Jim rubbed his torso against Mary's, as he turned her just enough to slide his left hand inside her panties. "You certainly are. I'm not exactly dry myself." As Jim started to withdraw his hand, Mary grasped his forearm. "Stay there. I love to have you touch me there." She turned her mouth to his again and their lips and tongues danced anew to their own sensual rhythm. Jim's left middle finger explored the outer boundaries of the mouth of her vagina, before advancing through her well-dampened public hairs to her swollen clitoris. As he tenderly touched her erection, she shuddered involuntarily, and her body seemed to go limp.

"Let's get more comfortable," Jim whispered. Sweeping her into his arms, he carried her into the training room. Earlier, he had brought in one of the cushioned mats used by the gymnastics team and placed it between the treatment table and the whirlpool. Two large towels were spread out on the mat, and several more were folded and stacked on one end.

Mary's smile broadened. "You sly devil."

"A football coach is nothing if not prepared," Jim countered. "You're going to love the whirlpool."

"I love you. That's what I love."

They explored the limits of their sexuality with sensuous abandon, oblivious of the passage of time, the chemistry of their interaction driving them to an ecstasy beyond their wildest dreams. It was well after dark, when Mary left the fieldhouse, and Jim began to put things back in order.

17

DISTASTEFUL DUTY

Lieutenant Louis Trosclair rang the doorbell of the Robicheaux residence on Turnbull. "Damn! Looks like nobody's home." He had observed the blue Omega in the drive, as he came up the walk and was hopeful that he could get on with the unpleasant assignment it had been his misfortune to draw. Returning to his squad car, he got Captain Kevin Jones on the radio.

"Captain, I'm at the Robicheauxs, but no one's here. I'll wait a while to see if she shows. Say 20:30. Unless you have any other ideas."

"Let's hope she shows. I'm sorry I had to call you out on Sunday evening."

"Forget it, Captain. My wife wanted me to take her and the kids to Bacchus tonight. At least I got out of that." "You're a good man, Lou. If she doesn't show by 21:00, call me back."

"10:4."

Lieutenant Trosclair lit a cigarette and steeled himself for what might be a long vigil. It was 20:40, when he observed a female figure walking briskly along the sidewalk. She wore a hooded sweatsuit. He came to full attention, when she turned into the Robicheaux driveway and disappeared around the side of the house. Within a minute, several lights came on inside. Stepping from his unit, he paused to brush his uniform and straighten his tie. The headlights of a pickup illuminated him, and he waited for it to pass before crossing the street.

"Well, what have we here?" the lieutenant said to himself. The truck slowed and pulled up along the curb opposite his unit. The driver hopped out, seemingly oblivious to his presence, and headed for the Robicheaux driveway.

"Just a minute, Sir." The Lieutenant hurried to catch up to him.

Jay Robicheaux turned to face the policeman just behind his mother's Omega. "Anything wrong, Officer?"

"I'm Lieutenant Trosclair from the Sheriff's Office. I need to talk to Mrs. Matthew Robicheaux. I saw you headed for the house, and I thought you might be of assistance. Do you live here?"

"Yes, Sir. You want my Mom."

"What's your name, Son?" The lieutenant extended his hand and felt the strength of Jay's grip.

"Jay. Jay Robicheaux. Wait by the front door. I'll get my Mom." Jay entered the house the way Mary had. Lieutenant Trosclair was glad that there would be someone like Jay around when he spoke to Mrs. Robicheaux. There was no telling how much support she might need this night but he expected that young man of hers could provide it.

"Come in, Lieutenant." Jay led the officer into the living room immediately to the right of the front door. "Sorry to keep you waiting. Mom had to change."

The lawman smiled knowingly. His wife wouldn't put out the garbage without checking her make-up he thought.

"Sit down," Jay invited. "Can I get you something to drink? Coffee maybe?"

"No, thanks."

The two men studied each other in the awkward silence that filled the moments, until Mary entered the room.

"Mom, this is Lieutenant Trosclair. Lieutenant, my Mom, Mary Robicheaux."

The policeman stood at attention and offered his hand to Mary. "Ma'am."

"Excuse me." Jay started to leave the room.

Lieutenant Trosclair stopped him, as he passed behind his mother. "Stay, Jay. This concerns you, too."

Mary's face, which had been all aglow, went ashen with anxiety.

"Ma'am, your husband has been hurt in a boating accident, and they've taken him to Ochsner."

"Ochsner? But, he was fishing way down near the Gulf." Mary looked confused.

"Ochsner is called in on nearly every serious accident in the Gulf or marsh. They have two medically equipped helicopters, and it's the fastest way," the lieutenant explained.

"He's hurt real bad, isn't he?" Mary felt faint.

"I have no detailed information. The Sheriff just sent me to drive you to the hospital, if necessary. You're to ask for Dr. Petrovich in emergency." The officer spoke reassuringly.

Mary was quivering now. Jay took her in his arms, and she buried her face in his chest. "Oh, God! Oh, no! Please, God." She began to sob piteously.

Jay hugged his mother gently and kissed her softly on top of her head. Without releasing his hold on Mary, Jay fixed his gaze on Lieutenant Trosclair and said calmly, "Thank you for your concern. I'll have her at Ochsner within the hour. That's Dr. Petrovich in emergency, right?"

"Right. I'm sorry for your trouble, Jay…Mrs. Robicheaux. If there is anything I can do, call me at this number." The lieutenant handed a business card to Jay. "I wrote the doctor's name on the back. I'll let myself out."

Jay nodded, and the lieutenant went out to his unit. As he turned south on Cleary, he made contact with Captain Jones. "Captain, I got the word to the Robicheaux woman. Her son is with her, and they'll be at Ochsner by 22:00."

"Good job, Lou. Go home and get some rest."

"Easy for you to say, Captain. Why the fuck doesn't the Department get a chaplain for this shit?" Like they have in Orleans! They don't pay us enough for this."

"Easy, Lou. You passed it off on the doctor, didn't you? They make enough."

"Yeah, I passed it off, Captain. But, they know. They always know."

18

THE WAKE

Michelle sat on one of the upholstered chairs against the wall, near the entrance to the small private salon that Leitz-Eagan reserved for the immediate family members of the deceased. The rows of folding chairs facing the casket were occupied by some fifty young men who sat with arms folded in respectful silence. Michelle knew most of them. They were Jay's upper classman teammates from Rummel. All of them wore varsity jackets. Michelle had watched Coach Boyle and Scott Weigand lead them into the parlor a few minutes earlier. Scott had carried a large wreath which the funeral director had positioned near the bier.

As her eyes wandered over the somber assemblage of young athletes, Michelle noticed that quite a few of them had black smudges on their foreheads, and her mind wandered to the traditional Ash Wednesday ceremony she had attended early that morning with her family. She envisioned Monsignor Bennett moving along the communion rail, smearing a blessed mixture of holy oils and ashes on the forehead of each kneeling penitent, repeatedly enjoining, "Remember, Man, that you are dust and into dust you shall return."

As Monsignor Bennett approached Michelle, the monotonous repetition of his admonition seemed to hammer together all the sad events of the two days following the "return to dust" of Jay's father. She had spent most of those 48 hours with Jay and his mother.

Mary had broken down often and cried forlornly, but Jay had held it together, attending to the plethora of problems death brings to a family. Though he shed not a tear, Michelle knew intuitively that Jay's agony far exceeded that of his mother. Mary was weeping more for herself than grieving for Matt. Her tryst with Coach Boyle weighed heavily on her conscience.

Jay had kept his grief bottled up inside until late Mardi Gras night. Then, as he held Michelle in a parting embrace outside his house, he could no longer hide his pain. Michelle felt his great chest shudder spasmodically, and his soft mournful sobs pierced her soul like a two-edged sword. Not a word was spoken as she held him close, sharing his sorrow, until he regained his composure.

Now, as she tilted her head back to receive her ashes, the thought of Jay's suffering overwhelmed her. She felt a massive solitary tear glide down her right cheek. She had shed three tears in her life she thought. All over Jay. When he lost a game. Then a scholarship. Now a father. This last tear was the first to be seen by another.

Monsignor Bennett's hands had trembled as he placed the ashes on her forehead, and he uttered the ritual words unintelligibly, as he looked down on her face. After a moment's hesitation, her visibly shaken confessor had moved on to service the long line of waiting parishioners.

"Michelle." Jay's light touch on her arm snapped her eyelids open, and she returned to the present reality of Matt Robicheaux's wake. "I'd like you to meet Mr. Peter Hensley and his wife, Betty. They were customers of my father from our neighborhood." Nothing in the demeanor of Jay or Betty indicated that they had shared Betty's bed just last Friday.

"I'm pleased to meet you though I wish it were under happier circumstances." Michelle offered her hand to them.

"Yes, it's too bad about Matt. You just never know, do you?" Betty said.

No one spoke for a while, and the silence became uncomfortable for everyone.

"Come on. I'll show you where to get some coffee and sandwiches," Jay offered.

"We hope to see you again, Michelle," Pete said, as he moved away with Jay and Betty.

"Thank you," Michelle replied.

After they sat with their coffee at a small table in the hospitality room, Pete said to Jay, "Michelle is beautiful." Then turning to Betty, he said, "Isn't she, Honey?"

Betty nodded slightly. "She certainly is."

Jay established a solid eye contact with the Hensleys, before he said, "She's more than that. Without her, I don't know how my mom and I would have made it through this."

No one said anything for a minute. Finally, Jay stood and said, "I better get back to Mom. Thanks for coming."

Pete rose and shook Jay's hand. "Later, when things settle, come and see me about the job. I think you'd be perfect."

Jay lowered his gaze toward the floor. "Thanks."

19

THE MANRESA DECISION

"Mom, I'm not sure I should go," Jay said. Mary and Jay were sitting in the Robicheaux den the morning after they buried Matt. "Go, Jay. Go. Now, more than ever, you should go. I need to be alone for a while," Mary said.

"I don't know, Mom," Jay said with concern.

"Don't worry about me. I'll be fine. And you know Michelle will be checking on me. Matter of fact, she's coming over tomorrow to help me go through some of Daddy's things. We'll put together some boxes for the Goodwill." She sighed and continued, "God rest his soul. He never threw anything away." Mary took Jay's hands in hers and looked him straight in the eye. "I know how close you were to him. You need some time in a setting like Manresa."

"I suppose you're right, Mom. OK. I'll call Mr. Delaune and tell him I'm still going."

"Good." Mary got up and headed for her bedroom. "I'm going to lie down a while. If I'm not up by noon, knock on my door."

"OK. Look. Pull the phone jack in your room, and I'll turn down this one." After Mary shut her bedroom door, Jay adjusted the ringer volume on the phone in the den to its minimum, before he dialed Joe Delaune's business number.

"Mr. Delaune, it's Jay. You asked me at the wake to call you before 10:30 about the retreat. Well, I talked it over with my mom, and we decided it's best if I go."

"Swell, Jay! I'll pick you up at 4:40. How is your mother?"

"She's got it together again. She hasn't cried since they gave her the flag at the grave site. Michelle can tell you. You can believe Michelle would have stayed with her last night, if mom needed any help. So, she really is OK. Just needs some rest."

"Glad to hear it. How about you, Jay? Are you looking forward to Manresa?"

"It seemed like a good idea, when you told me about it last Saturday, but I'm not sure what I'm getting into."

"Just go with an open mind. Don't put any pressure on yourself to accomplish anything…except to relax. You can sleep all you want, and the food is great."

"Well, now, I think I might be pretty good at this retreat stuff after all."

Joe laughed and said, "You'll enjoy it, Jay. I'm glad you could join us. Zeke Fielding, a tennis buddy of mine, will be riding with us. Any questions?"

"No Sir. I'll be ready to go at 4:30. Thanks again, Mr. Delaune."

"Don't mention it. So long for now."

20

SUNDAY AFTERNOON COFFEE

"Well, Ann, what's the story on Michelle?" Monsignor Bennett sat across the table from Ann Delaune. He was in the same chair Michelle always used when she and Ann had their private late-night conversations.

"I really didn't think I'd get back to you this quickly. As you know, we really had to start with a medical exam, and, as we agreed in our conversation Wednesday, we didn't want Michelle to know we were concerned. I was thinking it would be months before I could swing it, and here it is only Sunday…less than a week since you called me about Michelle's 'big tear'."

"Good grief, Ann!" Monsignor Bennett interrupted. "Just tell me what you found out. Is my sweet angel OK?"

"She's OK, John." Ann hesitated. The Monsignor had sat and enjoyed coffee and conversation with her on many a Sunday afternoon, but he had never cut her short. She wasn't sure if she should elaborate without waiting for the priest's lead. It came quickly.

"I'm sorry I interrupted you, Ann. I've just been so worried, since I saw that big tear flow down Michelle's cheek, and it struck me that I had never seen her cry in all these years. Please fill me in."

"She had a complete physical and psychological profile done Friday. The Tulane tennis coach called me Thursday morning about Michelle's scholarship, and it came up that she would need a physical. I asked if he could arrange it Friday or Saturday, since Michelle was out of school, and Jay was at Manresa. He set it up for 8:30 Friday morning." Ann paused for a sip of her coffee. The Monsignor waited patiently.

"I spoke to the ophthalmologist privately. A Dr. Rivera. Nice man. He used a lot of medical terms. Lachrymal this. Lachrymal that. He said Michelle had all the right stuff. He found from this special scanning devise that Michelle's eyes emit a lot more heat than normal. He thinks this explains why Michelle doesn't cry tears…at least, not often. Something about the rate of evaporation offsetting the rate of secretion. He said she might produce a tear or two under the influence of very intense sadness or joy.

The psychologist confirmed that Michelle's lack of tears wasn't due to a personality problem. His name is Matthews. He said Michelle was as perfect a balance of temperaments as he had ever seen and that she was very empathetic. So. Do you feel better, John?"

"Very much so. On hindsight, I think I may have overreacted, but Michelle is so special to me."

"Would you like some more coffee?"

"No, thanks. What time is Joe coming home?"

"He should be back by 5:00. He has to drop off Jay and Zeke first."

"Where is Michelle?"

"She went to see Jay's mom for a while and to wait for Jay at his house."

"Well, Ann. Thanks for the coffee. And the good news. I'll be on my way. I'm glad that Michelle passed her physical with flying colors!"

"Not exactly, John. Her urine test pointed to a mild bladder infection. The doctor gave her a prescription and said it should clear up quickly. He'll run another test in a month to follow up."

"Keep me posted. Give my best to Joe."

21

AN UNSETTLED MIND

Mary Robicheaux lay on her back on the bed she had shared with Matt for twenty years. She was glad to be alone at last, though she appreciated the support she received through the ordeal of Matt's death and funeral. Jay and Michelle had been her pillars of strength, but now they were gone. Jay had left at 4:30 for Manresa, and Michelle had stayed with her until 6:30. She had convinced Michelle that she would be fine, but Michelle insisted she would come back to check on her Friday, after she finished her medical check-up for Tulane.

Mary glanced at the red LED display of the clock-radio on her dresser. 8:37 pm. She would have all night and most of Friday to begin to try to make some sense of what Matt's death would mean to the rest of her life. For all the passion Matt had shown her over the last 10 years, their marriage had died.

She wondered if the memories that kept flashing before her mind's eye would ever slow to a normal pattern that could complement a chain of thought. The images that kaleidoscoped through her consciousness triggered feelings that ran the gamut of the emotional spectrum. The visions were clear, but fleeting and chaotic in their flow, their accompanying emotions clashing like discordant notes. They did not allow her to settle into any mood, but kept her immersed in a feeling of uneasiness.

There was only one image that Mary could sustain. She had forced it from her consciousness a thousand times since Sunday night, not feeling she had the right to entertain it…or it her. Now, as the memory of Jim Boyle's kisses set her body tingling, she noted the red LED readout in the darkened bedroom. 8:46 pm. She knew that whatever she did with the rest of her life, it had to be with Jim. He had her heart. She could never keep him from her mind. Mary reached for the bedside phone and rang Jim Boyle's number.

"Boyle."

"Hello, Jim. Can you talk?" There was a long silence. "Jim, are you still there?"

"Mary! I'm surprised to hear from you just now is all. But, delighted. Yeah, I'm by myself. I'm so glad you called. I've been wondering how you're doing and feeling helpless to do you any good. I was feeling down, thinking it might be a while before I got to talk to you."

"I'm OK. It just occurred to me how much I miss you." She paused for several seconds. "I need you, Jim. Can you come over?"

"What? I mean…when?…No…where? Your house?"

Mary relished the excitement in Jim's voice. "Jim, I mean now. My house."

"Mary, sounds great, but do you think it's wise?"

"Jay's gone to Manresa and I'm alone with only night lights on in the house."

"We'll have to be really careful."

"Park by Rummel and walk over. Come through the empty lot behind my house, and I'll let you in through the patio door. The gate in the back fence is unlocked."

"I'll be at your patio door by 9:30. I love you."

"And I love you."

22

MEDITATING AT MANRESA

At first, Jay did not recognize the voice that whispered his name. Joe Delaune had knocked softly, but insistently, at the door to his room in the main building at Manresa. His voice carried easily through the open transom. "Jay! Are you OK?"

The springs of Jay's bed creaked, as Jay sat up and swung his legs over the side of his mattress. Joe waited quietly now, realizing he had succeeded in rousing Jay.

"That you, Mr. Delaune?" Jay asked sleepily. "Come on in. It's not locked."

"Look, I'm sorry if I disturbed you." Joe started into the room, but stopped when he swung the door wide enough to see that Jay was clad only in his jockey shorts, which were bulging outward with the full erection of a larger than average penis. It was only nature's way of helping the male species control a full bladder during sleep, but it evoked an involuntary stare from Joe.

Jay's eyes followed Joe's line of sight to his crotch, and he said without any hint of embarrassment, "Yeah, I got to get to the bathroom." Joe was embarrassed that he had allowed himself to stare at the nearly naked young man before him, but Jay could not have cared less. "Look, Jay. I didn't see you at the morning meditation and…well, that didn't concern me. But, when you weren't at breakfast, I thought maybe you were sick. I…"

Jay cut in with a wave of his right hand. "I'm fine. I just overslept. I guess I meditated too much last night." Jay rose to his full height and stretched, reaching toward the ceiling and yawning. He took one stride forward and bent over the wash basin against the wall. "Look, I'll see you at dinner," Joe said, as he began to back into the hall.

Jay had already splashed cold water on his head and face and was reaching for a towel. "Thanks for looking in on me, Mr. Delaune. I might have slept through dinner, too." Jay chuckled, and Joe's face relaxed into a smile as he closed the door to Jay's room.

Joe thought to himself, "Poor kid, he must be worn out from the trauma of last week."

"Boy! Do I need to tap a kidney!" Jay thought aloud, as he reached the commode. As he urinated, he fondled his diminishing erection and said to himself, "This old dick has got me into some tight spots, but it just got me out of one. Old Joe was so busy gawking at it, he never came far enough into the room to smell the beer on my breath."

As soon as he finished at the commode, Jay returned to the basin, where he brushed his teeth and gargled with Scope. He hadn't dared to run the water when he had come in at 3:45 that morning. It was a real adventure to sneak back to his room in this creaky antebellum building, without disturbing his fellow retreatants. Fortunately, their snoring masked the slight unavoidable noises he made. He had to grin at himself in the mirror, as he gripped his razor. "What a night!" he thought.

Jay had felt ready to explode after two nights and two days of the retreat atmosphere. Everyone observed the rule of silence and stayed to themselves. Some spent time between scheduled exercises walking the spacious grounds of the beautifully landscaped old plantation. Some sat on benches under the centuries old oaks. Others spent the time inside in their room, the library, or the chapel. They read religious books or pamphlets, listened to inspirational tapes or fingered rosary beads. The phone was only available for emergencies. Furthermore, there were no TVs or radios…no newspapers or secular magazines. By Saturday evening, Jay had decided he had to have a break, before he became a basket case.

At 10:15 that night, he had slipped off the property via the gravel road used by the working staff. After the evening conference in the chapel, he had simply waited in the deep shadows of a huge oak next to a point where the access road met the River Road, the state highway that followed the curves of the east bank of the Mississippi River. While waiting until nearly every light in the main building went out, he remembered stopping at a Time Saver on the way to Manresa the previous Thursday. Joe Delaune and Zeke Fielding had wanted to buy cigarettes. He thought he could walk there in twenty minutes, if he didn't catch a ride.

Jay slowly shook his head and smiled at his image in the mirror, as he recalled how short his walk had been. He had progressed only about 200 yards along the winding River Road, when a red Camaro came out of the curve just behind him, forcing him to leave the narrow shoulder and jump the drainage ditch at the base of the levee. The driver had taken the curve a little too fast and had skidded onto the shoulder. Jay watched the right rear wheel slip into the ditch, just as the vehicle slid to a stop. The engine stalled and Jay heard the grind of the starter restoring it to action. He leaped back over the ditch and headed toward the mired Camaro. Jay could see that the driver was not getting anywhere. There was a street lamp just across the road from the car, and Jay could see its occupants clearly as he came abreast of it.

"You girls having trouble?" Jay smiled, flashing his best expression of concern.

The driver stopped gunning the engine and looked up at Jay. "I hope to hell you're some fucking knight in shining armor, cause we sure as hell are two damsels in distress."

"I'm the poor bastard you just ran off the road." Jay's expression shifted to a disapproving glare.

"I'm sorry, Sir. You OK?" The driver put her right hand to her mouth. Jay had knocked her off balance and assumed control of the situation.

"I'm fine, but you girls are in a dangerous position." Jay's expression was one of friendly concern again. "Do you have a flashlight?"

The driver nodded toward the girl in the front passenger seat, who fumbled in the glove compartment and extracted a flashlight. She handed it to the driver, who passed it to Jay. "What are you going to do with the light?" the driver inquired.

"Nothing. I want you to walk back to the start of the curve and swing it back and forth to warn off anybody that might drive the way you do." Jay opened the door for the driver. As soon as she got out, Jay handed her the flashlight and slid behind the steering wheel. Jay activated the hazard warning lights. As he shifted the Camaro into reverse, he noticed that the driver was still alongside the car. "Come on, Sweetheart," Jay said. "Get your buns up the road and wave that light. I don't want some nut driving up my ass, while I'm rocking this baby loose."

Jay cut the wheel hard right and backed up slowly, angling the stuck rear wheel against the side of the ditch and moving the right front away from its soft edge. When the left rear wheel was precariously close to the ditch, Jay gunned the car forward. It trembled and shook free. Jay had checked that no cars were coming, because he knew he would cross both lanes as he fired loose. After straightening out the car, Jay backed it toward the light swinging at the start of the curve behind him.

"Need a lift?" Jay grinned at the girl with the flashlight.

"No, good-looking, I've got a car. But, I wouldn't mind being picked up by you."

"Get in. I'll just drive to the Time Saver up ahead, if you don't mind. That's where I was headed."

"Be our guest. We were going there to pick up my older sister." She got in on the passenger side as the other girl slid over net to Jay.

"I'm Jay. Who are you fine young ladies?" Jay asked as he eased the Camaro forward.

"I'm Josie," the girl next to Jay said with a giggle.

"And I'm Connie," the other added. "We're cousins. First cousins."

"Do you go to school around here?" Jay asked.

"I'm a senior at Lutcher. Josie's a junior." Connie pulled her knees up against her bosom, and her short denim skirt slipped up to her panty line.

"Y'all had a great football team last year. At least in Triple-A," Jay offered.

"Hell, we make the playoffs every year long as I can remember," Connie commented. "You look like a football player. Did you play in high school?"

"Yeah. A little." Jay didn't want to correct their assumption that he was out of high school or reveal too much about himself, so he switched the subject with a question. "What do y'all do for fun around here on a Saturday night?"

Josie giggled again, but Connie replied. "Unless there's a dance, we ain't got much but private parties here abouts."

Jay smiled. "There's the Time Saver." He pulled the Camaro to a smooth stop right in front of the entrance. "Thanks for the lift."

"Thank you. We'd still be in the fucking ditch if you hadn't come along." Connie accepted the keys Jay held out to her.

Jay was amused by Connie's vulgarity. It seemed as natural to her as her heavy Cajun accent. He held the door for the girls as they entered the store. Jay headed straight toward the beverage coolers. The girls engaged in an animated conversation with the cashier, turning frequently to gaze in Jay's direction. The cashier must be Connie's older sister thought Jay. Now, there was a good looking woman. He hoped Connie was saying something that would put him on her good side.

As Jay moved toward the check-out counter, Connie and Josie hurried outside. "Where're they headed?" Jay asked the cashier.

"They're gassing up my car. I'm Leslie. Connie's my little sister. Look, I owe you one for helping them back there." She smiled and Jay knew from the look in her beautiful deep blue eyes that he was definitely on her good side.

"I'm kind of lost in these parts. Do you know where a man might be able to enjoy a few drinks, maybe dance a little, enjoy some music?"

"Honey, I'm in the same mood as you, but I ain't lost. I know every honky tonk in the river Parishes." Leslie paused to observe a black woman come through the door. "That's Mabel. My relief. She'll let you hang around till I get back. Give me a half-hour to dump the kids and then…'Laissez les bons temps roullez'."

Jay's smile widened as he reached this point in his revelry. He had finished shaving and backed away from the mirror to lie back on his bed. This bed wasn't nearly as comfortable or roomy as Leslie's he thought. He chuckled aloud, as he recalled Leslie telling him not to waste Thursday and Friday nights if he made the retreat again. He recalled that the retreat master had suggested in his welcoming address that they take notes and formulate a resolution. "Well," Jay said to himself, "as far as notes go, I wrote down Leslie's number…and as for a resolution, I sure as hell am going to call it."

23

PROM NIGHT

"Jay, I have to go back to the house."

"Okay. Forget something?" Michelle never looked lovelier to him, and Jay was not going to let a small delay dampen his euphoric mood. It was senior prom night. He was wearing the Colombian blue tuxedo his class selected for their last formal dance, and Michelle had on an emerald green strapless evening gown.

"I have to use the bathroom."

Jay turned his mother's blue Omega around in the Paradise Manor parking lot and reversed his direction on Sauve Road, heading back to Michelle's house, which they had left not three minutes earlier.

"Michelle, is it my imagination or are you going to the bathroom more than you used to?"

"It's not your imagination. I've been fighting a bladder infection off and on since Lent started, and I just seem to have to go more often. Maybe, it's the medication I'm taking for it. Been on it over two months. Since my Tulane physical, in fact. I'm going to ask my doctor about it. Anyway, I feel great tonight." "You look great, too."

As Jay turned right off of busy Sauve Road onto Tiffany, his path was suddenly blocked by a maroon Mustang, which screeched to a stop well over into Jay's half of the side street. Michelle gasped as Jay was forced to slam on his brakes. Jay glared angrily at the driver of the Mustang, a husky man of about 25. He appeared not to have shaven for a week, and his straight dirty blond hair was tied back in a pony tail with a thick rubber band. The man in the front passenger seat could have been a thinner version of the driver's twin. There was a steady stream of traffic on the busy street behind him, and Jay could not back up. The driver of the Mustang could have easily backed up on the idle side street, but he stayed put, effectively blocking Jay's progress.

"Michelle, step out and wait on the sidewalk till I call you back. I don't want you in the car if we get rear-ended," Jay said very calmly. "What are you going to do?" Michelle asked with a worried expression. She knew Jay had a temper.

"I'm just going to ask them to move. Maybe, they don't realize I can't back up as easily as they can." Jay put the Omega in park and got out on the driver's side. Michelle exited the passenger side and walked toward the sidewalk.

As Jay covered the short gap between the Omega and the Mustang, his mood was rapidly deteriorating from euphoria to rage. As he reached the left front door of the Mustang, the driver reached through the opened window and poured the remains of a can of Budweiser onto the street. The contents splashed onto Jay's dress shoes and the cuffs of his tuxedo. Jay was ready to explode but struggled mightily to keep his cool. He didn't want to ruin a special night for Michelle.

The driver only added fuel to the fire, "What's the matter, Pretty Boy? Is your little slut leaving you?" the driver asked.

It was all Jay could do not to yank the driver through the window, but his choice of words did nothing to defuse the confrontation. "Back up, asshole," Jay ordered. His icy stare froze the driver, and his bravado waned. His companion hadn't been exposed to Jay's icy stare and remained combative. He leaned between the steering wheel and the driver, and challenged, "Who you calling an asshole?!"

Without blinking, Jay leaned down and lowered his face to window level and said, "Well, now, I'm not sure. You're so close together it's hard to tell the asshole from the pussy." Fueled by adrenaline, the passenger burst from his side of the Mustang and raced around the front of the car to engage Jay. He ran into a textbook right forearm shiver that knocked him toward the front of Jay's vehicle. He landed, dazed, on his back, as Jay bent over to finish any ability he had to continue the fight. No need for that, his attacker was unconscious, but had he not bent over at that moment, he probably would have been struck by one or more of the three bullets that whizzed over his back. Instead, two of them struck Michelle in her abdomen, and she slumped to the sidewalk with an agonizing scream. It's hard to say whether it was Michelle's scream or the simultaneous arrival of two Jefferson Parish police cars that so rattled the driver of the Mustang that he dropped the gun that he had fired at Jay through the driver's side window. Within seconds, some half dozen deputies had what was a crime scene completely contained.

24

LIEUTENANT TROSCLAIR RETURNS

Lou Trosclair was part of the initial wave of deputies that arrived on the scene. He happened to know Joe Delaune from his frequent use of the Little Farms tennis courts. They occasionally got into pick-up doubles games there, and he had often seen Joe working out with his daughter, Michelle. As luck would have it, he had also been the deputy assigned to inform Mary Robicheaux of Matt's accident in the marsh, and Jay had left a lasting impression on him. Deputy Trosclair had all he could handle to get Jay to release Michelle, whom he had cradled in his arms where she fell. "C'mon, Jay. Let the EMTs help her. She's going into shock." The blood stain on Michelle's gown was spreading rapidly.

"An ambulance will take her to Ochsner, Jay," the deputy reassured. Observing the blood splattered over the right sleeve of Jay's tuxedo, the deputy commented, "It looks like you're hurt, too."

Jay responded, "That's not my blood."

"Good", thought the deputy. "We'll only need two ambulances." The man lying in the street was in obvious need of medical attention.

Jay gave the short version of what had transpired to Lieutenant Trosclair and was allowed to ride with Michelle to the Ochsner emergency suite. This arrangement conflicted with SOP, but the Captain owed his deputy one, since that fateful day when Matt Robicheaux was killed. Trosclair had to agree to keep Jay under surveillance until relieved. If necessary, Jay must be available to answer any further questions.

That scenario sure beat the one that would likely have unfolded had he attempted to forcibly separate Jay from Michelle. Jay rode in the ambulance with Michelle but had to sit out of the way, while two EMTs fought to stabilize her. Lieutenant Trosclair escorted the ambulance to Ochsner with his unit's lights and siren blazing. Enroute he radioed the 4th District to arrange for an officer to contact Michelle's parents to inform them that she was being transported to Ochsner, a victim of multiple gunshot wounds.

25

THE MEN IN THE MUSTANG

The driver of the Mustang was arrested on the spot and brought to the Jefferson Parish lock-up on Airline Highway in a squad car. Deputies investigating the scene had quickly determined that the Mustang was stolen, and that the driver had warrants out on him from St. Landry Parish. His name was Joseph Boustany. He was a convicted felon on parole. Just to possess a firearm was a violation of his parole, but he had used it to fire shots that had struck a young girl, whose life now hung by a thread. Joseph had panicked when his companion had been knocked to the pavement by Jay, just as he was surrounded by squad cars. He continued to panick under the intense interrogation of his captors. He sang like a bird, without availing himself of his rights to remain silent and have an attorney present. He thought to get some reduction on the charges they could bring against him in return for his cooperation. It wouldn't be the first or last time a guilty plea would purchase a reduction in charges from the State. He revealed the name of his companion to be Peter Ortego. His identification of his companion in the Mustang helped speed things along, as Peter was unable to be interrogated. He was in a coma at Ochsner.

26

THE PROGNOSIS

It was the morning after the Rummel prom, when Dr. Timothy White met with Jay and Michelle's parents. Dr. White had been in surgery, attempting to assess and repair the damage done to Michelle by two .38 caliber bullets. It was now 6:00 am, nine hours after Michelle was prepped.

After introductions were exchanged, Dr. White began. "I was able to repair damage to her bladder and large intestine, but the damage to her kidneys will require dialysis to replace their function."

"Are there any other options?" Ann Delaune inquired.

"Our other option would be to do a kidney transplant, but to do so would require that we first combat a serious case of sepsis, and then find a donor kidney with a good match. But, we're getting ahead of ourselves. Unless we get her on renal dialysis now, she will die of kidney failure. I collected samples of spillage from her bladder and large intestine, while cleaning them up. These will be analyzed to determine the best antibiotics to fight the bacteria in them."

"Can we see her, Doctor White?" Ann inquired.

"It will be awhile, I'm afraid. She is still in surgery. I called in our top vascular surgeon to implant a fistula in her left forearm so she can be attached to a renal dialysis machine. Moreover, she is in a medically induced coma to keep her from thrashing about…and to spare her as much pain as possible. It may be a few days before any but medical personnel may approach her. She is in a sterile environment in an isolated intensive care unit."

As Doctor White excused himself, he cautioned, "Get some rest and advise family and well-wishers that Michelle will not be allowed to have visitors at least until she is released from ICU."

"Is there anything we can do, Doctor?" It was Ann asking in a piteous voice.

"Pray," the doctor suggested.

27

JAY'S REACTION

Jay had followed Michelle on her gurney ride from the ambulance to a point just outside the triage area, where he was forced to release her hand and turn back. He had been directed to a waiting area. There an admissions clerk had attempted to get from him the basic information concerning Michelle. With a blank stare, he had given her the number of Ann Delaune.

The clerk left for a few minutes. When she returned, she informed Jay that Ann and Joe Delaune were enroute. Joe Delaune spotted Jay as soon as he entered the waiting room of the emergency suite. He was seated with his elbows on his knees, hands covering his face, the right sleeve of his blue tux splattered with blood. "Jay! What happened?"

"I'm so sorry. Some punk shot Michelle." Jay handed Joe a card Lieutenant Trosclair had left with him. "This cop will have the complete report of what happened by some time tomorrow. Michelle is in surgery now."

An admissions clerk had been waiting for the Delaunes to arrive and now addressed Joe and Mary. "Mr. and Mrs. Delaune? I'm sorry to interrupt, but I need to get more information on your daughter."

Jay was thankful for the interruption. It was painful for him to face the Delaunes. He felt responsible for what had happened to their daughter, and his helplessness to do anything for Michelle weighed on him like a ton of bricks. It was nearly 10 pm, when the Delaunes approached Jay. "We're going to another waiting area where the surgeon will report to us when he finishes his work." Jay followed them without a word to a new waiting room, and there they stayed until they were briefed on Michelle's condition at 6 am. Dr. White's parting suggestion to them had been "Pray!"

At a complete loss as to doing anything helpful, while at the same time wanting to do everything possible, Jay's mind focused laser-like on Doctor White's suggestion, "Pray."

28

CRYING IN THE CHAPEL

Family and friends of the Delaunes began to add to the number of people in the surgery waiting area, just as Dr. White had made his original report on Michelle's condition. For Joe and Mary, there was no escaping their questions. Jay avoided all questions by quietly slipping out of the room. "Pray! Pray! Pray!" He said to himself. He found his way to the non-denominational chapel provided by the hospital for staff and visitors. The lighting in the chapel was subdued, except for a bright spotlight that illumined a large cross at the head of the room. Jay was glad to note that there were no other visitors. He desired to talk to no one but God and Michelle. He knelt on the first prie-dieu in the rear of the chapel.

"Lord, I know I'm a son-of-a bitch, but Michelle is an angel. I've come to love her, and I want to learn to love you like she does. Those bullets she took were meant for me, and I wish they had hit me instead of her. I'm going to go to confession to Father Mac over at Children's Hospital and start studying and practicing my Catholic faith. Michelle's love and example have changed me. I never want to be the same skirt-chasing, hell-raising son-of-a-bitch I've been. Please help me. I am in no position to place any conditions on your helping Michelle get well but please, please bring her back to me. Knowing Michelle, I'll add 'if you will.'"

Jay continued reflecting on his life. What a waste of time it had been. He had spent it on such unimportant things. By far the best thing in his life had been Michelle. The thought of losing her was unbearable, and his eyes filled with tears, which overflowed down his cheeks. Guilt weighed heavily on him for his infidelity at Manresa. He continued to reflect and pray in pretty much the same manner, until he felt a hand on his left shoulder about 10:00 am.

29

END OF A LONG VIGIL

Three weeks had elapsed since Michelle had been shot. Jay had spent nearly all of that time in the waiting room, nearest to where Michelle was being kept. The only exception was the time he spent in the chapel just down the hall. It made it easy for the nurses to find him, and he wanted to be available as soon as Michelle could be seen. A team of horses couldn't drag Jay from Ochsner, as long as Michelle's life hung in the balance.

Every other day, Mary, accompanied by Coach Boyle, had brought him an overnight bag with some toiletries, some underwear, and a pair of Rummel warmups. He used his well-practiced charm with the nurses, in what was a switch for him, not to get in their panties, but to obtain small favors. They were in great admiration of his devotion to Michelle.

In the wee hours, they tipped him off when rooms were unoccupied, so he could take a quick shower and change. They also brought him meals put together from the trays patients left untouched. He looked a lot better than he had when he first entered the waiting salon in his bloodied prom tuxedo.

Dr. Blom entered the waiting room accompanied by a team of two other physicians and several nurses at 9:00 am, on the fourth Sunday since Michelle's first surgery. Dr. Blom was the lead physician directing Michelle's treatment. He immediately spotted the now familiar figure of Jay seated in an overstuffed chair. Jay was reading the story of the conversion of St. Augustine from a book Father Mac had dropped off to him.

Augustine's conversion had begun when he had by chance opened a Bible to Romans 13: 13 – 14. It read: "Not in carousing and drunkenness, not in sexual excess and lust, not in quarreling and jealousy. Rather, put on the Lord Jesus Christ, and make no provision for the desires of the flesh." Jay could not help but think that the love and example of Michelle had moved him like the love and example of Augustine's mother had moved Augustine.

Putting his book aside, Jay stood and grasped Dr. Blom's hand, as he had done dozens of times during his long vigil. Dr. Blom directed his team to take a break while he updated Jay on Michelle. Dr. Blom then told Jay, "Follow me, Jay" and led him to a small private conference room just past the nearby chapel.Jay sensed that Dr. Blom did not have good news. His reports had been progressively negative. His instinct was correct.

 "Jay," Dr. Blom began, "Normally, I would have waited for Michelle's parents to get here, before I delivered the news I have for you, but you are so special to Michelle I couldn't take the chance that she might die without seeing you again and possibly talking to you. The only word I or my staff has heard her say has been your name."

"So, Michelle is dying?"

"Jay, we've done everything we can to save her. We could keep her alive on dialysis but we have lost the battle to control the infection that has spread throughout her blood and tissues. She is rapidly nearing total organ failure."

"Can I at least see her?"

"Maybe. But, not right away. I want to tell her parents what I've told you. With their permission, I plan to move her to our Hospice unit. We can make her more comfortable there, and possibly she'll be able to see and speak to her loved ones. We'll have her heavily sedated against the pain caused by her sepsis. They will definitely be able to be by her side, at least…and she may, from time to time, open her eyes and mouth a few words. I'm convinced that she'll haunt me from the grave, if I don't give you and her the chance to say goodbye."

"Let me know when you move her, and I'll follow right behind."

30

HOSPICE

The room in the hospice wing was more like a hotel suite than a hospital room. It contained sofas and recliners that could be converted into beds for guests who would stay overnight. It had a large walk-in closet and spacious bath. There were several large tables with matching chairs. Volunteers from Catholic Charities kept a refrigerator and cupboard well-stocked with food and drink for guests.

Jay waited just outside Michelle's suite until she was settled in her bed with all of her lines and monitors attached. When the nurses exited Michelle's room, Jay asked, "Is she settled in?" He didn't wait for a response. As Jay brushed by them, they protested, "Sir, wait! Dr. Blom hasn't quite finished updating Michelle's parents!"

Too late now. Jay was already by Michelle's side. He knew Joe and Mary and maybe others were on their way, but he wasn't waiting. He grasped her left hand gently. He hadn't touched her since prom night. "Michelle, Michelle, it's Jay" he said softly.

At the sound of Jay's voice a strange thing occurred. Michelle's face literally glowed, as though a dim light had been turned on. Then, she opened her eyes, which shone brightly. The smile in her eyes moved to her lips, and she spoke very softly but clearly, "Jay." Jay's heart was racing, as he bent closer to Michelle's lips in order to not miss any words she might manage. Jay heard every word, and they remained etched in his heart. He could never forget them. "I'm going to be with God. I want you to do something."

"Anything, my Darling!"

"Get and stay as close to God as you can, so I can still be close to you." Michelle closed her eyes, but her smile and the aura that had engulfed her visage remained. Jay knew she was gone. With tears streaming down his cheeks, he bent over her and smothered her forehead with kisses, repeating over and over, "I will. I will. I will." That is how Joe and Ann found them.

Dr. Brom said it was a miracle that Michelle had spoken and opened her eyes. He couldn't bring himself to chide Jay for not waiting for Michelle's parents. Jay was all she had on her mind during her long ordeal, and God did not deny her a last farewell to her beloved Jay. "What's that song?" he thought. "No two people have ever been so in love?"

31

AFTERMATH

Throughout Michelle's wake and funeral, those who knew him well saw in Jay a new persona. He appeared lost in thought, but he was far from that. Michelle had given him a mission, and he was just working out in his mind the best way to fulfill it. He could afford to take his time and, through prayerful thought, find his way to fulfill Michelle's dying directive. It was for him to be his life's work, and he was determined to get it right.

Matt had left a million-dollar life insurance payoff to Mary, and she didn't need for him to help support her. In fact, she offered to pay for his tuition to college and suggested he might want to try his hand at football as a walk-on. No one but Father Mac knew that Jay was a profoundly changed man. Father Mac had met with Matt for many hours, and through the knowledge he gained was the only one with any sense of the path Jay would take.

When six months had passed, Jay sat down with Mary and Jim Boyle to tell them he had made up his mind. It made it easy for him to leave town to find his way, since Mary and Jim were to be married. She would be well cared for by Coach Boyle…, and Jay had never seen her look at Matt like she looked at Jim.

Jay began, "My new life will take me to North Western Wyoming. I'll write you, when I get there. I've been given "directions as to what I need to bring, and I'll receive on the job training after I arrive."

"Going to be a cowboy?" Jim inquired.

"I don't want to talk about it at this point, Coach!" Coach knew not to press Jay by the expression on his face. "You can have my truck, Coach," Jay offered. "If you don't want it, I'll drive it out there and dispose of it, when I arrive. I wish you and Mom all the happiness in the world."

32

JAY KEEPS HIS PROMISE

When Jay arrived at the gates of the property, where he intended to spend the rest of his days, a man in a brown robe with a cowl met him at the gate. A sign on an arch over the gate read, "Welcome to Carmel." The man said, "You must be Jay Robicheaux, our new postulant."

"Yes, Sir"

"Tell me why you seek to join our order of cloistered and contemplative men."

"I want to get and stay as close to God as I can."

"I ask that question to every man that seeks to join us. That is the best answer I have received in 40 years."

ABOUT THE AUTHOR

If variety is the spice of life, John Hanson is well-seasoned. Born and raised in New Orleans, he has 181 undergraduate credits and holds a master's degree in physics and math from the University of Mississippi. He was even accepted for admission to the medical schools of the Universities of Louisville and Kentucky at the age of 37. He has been a teacher of every grade level from 7th to 12th, as well as lower division classes of physics for the University of Kentucky.

On the blue-collar side, he holds a diploma from the New Orleans Refrigeration School. On the white collar side, he earned licenses to sell real estate and insurance. He has been director of recruitment and training for one of the oldest moving and storage companies in America. He has been a deputy sheriff, as well as a private investigator. He was invited to try out with the Chicago Bears, Houston Oilers, and Dallas Cowboys.

His proudest achievement was his marriage of nearly 50 years to his angel, Patty, a registered nurse of extraordinary achievements. Being a Christian Brother ranks second.

BOOKS BY JOHN AND PATRICIA HANSON

Farewell to an Angel:
It All Began in Old New Orleans

John Hanson

9781606793435

Price: $24.95

The Cancer Journey: Hope & Inspiration

Patricia C. Hanson

9781606793572

Price: $19.95